THE BONUS DEAL

THE
BONUS DEAL

Archie Crail

Coteau Books

Edited by Ven Begamudré.

Cover painting, watercolour on paper, and frontispiece, ink on paper, by Emile Wilton.

Author photograph by Don Hall.

Cover and book design by Shelley Sopher, Coteau Books.

Typeset by Val Jakubowski, Coteau Books.

Printed and bound in Canada.

"Town and Country," "The New Man," "For One Pound a Day" (formerly titled "The Strike"), "Sometime for Sure," "The New Order" and "For My Diary" have been broadcast on CBC Radio's "Ambience." "Sharing a Trip to the Sea" was previously published in *Grain* (Fall 1991); "The New Man" was previously published in *Out of Place* (Coteau 1991).

The author wishes to thank the following individuals and institutions: Wayne Schmalz of CBC Radio for his wonderful support and infinite encouragement; Ven Begamudré and Connie Gault for their innovative suggestions during the editorial process; Geoffrey Ursell and Barbara Sapergia who recognised some of the stories in their infancy; all members of the Saskatchewan Writers Guild who, in various ways, assisted me; the Saskatchewan Arts Board for their generous assistance; the Coloured community of South Africa which gave me my first language, a perspective on the world and most of these stories; my parents, Brian and Sarah, who taught me how to tell stories; finally, to Denise, my wife, and my children Craig, Eldridge, St. Clair and Stanley—without you this would not have been possible.

The publisher gratefully acknowledges the financial assistance of the Saskatchewan Arts Board, the Canada Council, the City of Regina and Multiculturalism and Citizenship Canada.

Canadian Cataloguing in Publication Data

Crail, Archie, 1948-

The bonus deal

ISBN 1-55050-032-5 (bound) - 1-55050-031-7 (pbk.)

I. Title.

PS8555.R32B6 1992   C813'.54   C92-098017-1
PR9199.3.C72B6 1992

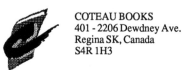

COTEAU BOOKS
401 - 2206 Dewdney Ave.
Regina SK, Canada
S4R 1H3

For Juffrou Madjiet
and Miss Pfaff

recommended.

CONTENTS

EARLY MAGIC

WE STARTED OFF QUITE EARLY IN THE MORNING. GRANDMA said this way we would avoid all the dust kicked up by passing vehicles later in the day.

I held onto her dress with one hand and trundled along to keep pace with her long, easy strides. Holding on like this I could keep up with her all day without getting left behind. Today she had put on a coarse, blue linen dress with lots of little white flowers. I liked this material because it was a nice rough fabric and my hand didn't slip or get sweaty as with her other silklike clothing. She had insisted I wear shoes for this outing. However, I had kicked up such a racket that she finally allowed me to go barefoot. Now she stopped so I could step into the powdery, dried clay which had collected in a few potholes. The clay had a sticky quality and I moved my toes about in absolute pleasure. This would've been impossible to do if I had worn shoes.

Nearby, Grandma sat under a low-growing olive tree and pinched a bit of chewing tobacco from her cigarette box. It was small, square and silver. She didn't seem in a great hurry. Once a month we went to collect her old age pension at the post office and, once or twice in between, she did a bundle of washing for a white family in town. This was my last year at home before starting school and I went everywhere she did. I looked for another pothole and wondered where exactly we were off to. Instead of asking, I decided that either way I would be in for a treat. If she was getting her pension money, then I would get a Coke and ice cream afterward. On the other hand, should there be washing to be done, then I would get the chance to play with the white children's many toys. Her sharp call of "Joseph!" shook me out of my musings. The farm road snaked like a pale brown ribbon behind us. We had come so far that, on looking back, I couldn't even see our white house between the distant rows of olive trees. A field mouse darted across the road and in the nearby grass a cricket was chirping. Otherwise we were the only people in sight. It was still early summer and the fragrance of peach blossoms wafted across from the other side of the road.

As we descended the last hill, the town lay below us—with its many buildings and bustling of people and vehicles. Today Grandma had no time for the dazzling display windows and their lifelike mannequins. She led me into a strange part of town with run-down buildings, smoking chimneys and from behind a wall, the clattering-thumping sounds of machinery. Once I saw men and women furiously packing things into boxes but felt too shy to ask Grandma what they were doing.

We arrived at a house I'd never seen. Near the front door three dirty, wind-blown children were pouring sand into soft drink bottles. A couple of bottles had artificial flowers stuck into them. A woman in a black dress opened the door for us. She was tall and gaunt and was smoking a cigarette.

I was totally surprised when Grandma called this woman by her first name, Margaret. Normally she would call white women *"ounooi," "klein nooi"* or just *"nooi."* All this accompanied by a little deference on Grandma's part. Now they were even hugging each other.

The woman disengaged herself from Grandma's embrace, puffed on the cigarette and shouted at the children:

"You bunch of rag tags! Come and meet your *aya* Anna!" The children looked up at us for a minute and then resumed their game.

From inside the house a spindly little creature, little taller than myself, came running out and immediately got lost in the folds of my grandmother's dress. After she had been sufficiently smothered and kissed, she came red-faced over to me. I was afraid she would want me to kiss her too. Embarrassed, I gave her a handshake.

"Come inside, Anna," the woman said, coughing a few times. "Come inside." Grandma went in with the oldest girl and her mother. I decided to help the other children fill the soft drink bottles instead.

After a while—filling the bottles and emptying them again—I wondered what was taking Grandma so long. When was she going to come outside and do the washing? I asked one of the children,

"Who does your washing for you?" but she ignored me.

Another child who had overheard the question said I was probably crazy. "Do you want to do our washing?" she asked of me. All three burst out laughing and added to my confusion.

I took a few furtive looks in the direction of the door and ignored the empty bottle that was handed to me. Summoning up my courage, I broke away from this futile activity and darted for the door. After I banged on it a few times, the eldest girl opened it. "Where's Ma?" I wanted to know. That's what I called Grandma.

Without letting me in, the girl turned and shouted into the house: "Ma! He wants you!"

"Who wants me?" came the hoarse, coughing reply.

"He, I mean this boy of *aya* Anna wants you!"

There wasn't even a hint of Ma's presence inside. I strained a peek past the little girl but got only a glimpse of her mother. Ma was rarely quiet and her thunderous voice dominated any conversation. Were these people playing some trick on me? I pushed the girl aside and barged in. Once inside the living-room, I realized Ma had abandoned me with this strange family. They weren't even Coloured. They were white and very poor. I looked about the room. Against one wall there stood a dusty display cabinet filled with all kinds of bric-a-brac. Some ornaments still had price tags on them. In a corner was a dining-room table, equally covered in black dust, and surrounded by six chairs. High up on a wall the ferocious head of some horned animal stared down at me. I felt so forlorn, so abandoned, that I wanted to burst into tears. Only the presence of the girl stopped me from doing so.

"Don't worry," the mother implored. "Your grandma will be back soon, little boy. You can play with Maria until she gets back."

I made no response.

"And what's your name?" she went on. "You can't play if you don't say your name."

"Joseph," I ventured.

She switched to a falsetto tone. "You mean your name's not Joey or Joe?"

"No," I said, "my name is Joseph."

"But you're a big boy," she said. She got a stick of candy cane from somewhere in the display cabinet. Getting close, she hugged me and gave me a piece. The smell of smoke from her clothing upset me so much that I started coughing.

"Do you have a cold?" she asked from a new height. "I'll give you some cough medicine. Just come with me to the kitchen."

I refused to follow her. Maria perched on one of the dining-room chairs and watched me worriedly. She looked like someone who had been taking care of siblings smaller than herself for a long time. Obviously I was beyond her abilities.

Presently her mother strode in with a large spoon and an even larger bottle. She filled the spoon with a dark brown liquid. "Come here, Joseph. Auntie will give you some medicine to make you feel better."

"But I'm not sick!" I protested. "I only want Ma!"

"Sure you don't want any?" She lowered herself to my level again.

"No!" I bawled unashamedly. "Where's Ma?"

"Well, if you don't want it, then I'll drink it myself." She swallowed the vile-looking stuff in one gulp, coughed a few times and replaced the cap. "Don't worry. Your grandma will be back soon."

A sudden tremor hit the house. The myriad ornaments clinked in the cabinet. The shuddering animal head on the wall seemed ready to gore me with one of its horns. I jumped with such a loud squeal that Maria and her mother broke into peals of laughter. This seemed to go on forever and, while they enjoyed their laughter, so I enjoyed my crying.

Maria was the first to recover from her laughter. "It's only the train, Joseph," she said. "It's only the train. You want to come and look for yourself?" She got up from the chair and motioned toward the kitchen while her mother, wiping the tears from her eyes, still guffawed.

Suddenly the mother had enough of this bawling. With quick, deft movements she gave me a flurry of spanks on the bottom. "Take him outside, Maria! I'm sick of this crying baby!"

The girl put her spindly arms around my shoulders and half dragged me out the kitchen door. Outside, an amazing sight met my tear-filled gaze. Starting right under the back door and stretching into the distance, there were rows upon rows of gleaming silver rails. At one end of the rails a steam engine shunted railcars while a little, old man in soiled coveralls waved two different coloured flags at the driver. The afternoon sun felt warm.

"Come close, Joseph," Maria's bright voice called. "Come

with me." She took me by the hand and showed how easy it was to jump from one rail to the next without stepping on the ties. I followed hesitantly.

Soon the engine started heading back in our direction. After criss-crossing a few lines, it chugged along on the very same rails we stood on. I felt the vibration in the rail and jumped onto the ground.

"Just stay here, Joseph," Maria said laughingly, "and you can feel the cool steam spray as it passes."

I wasn't prepared to take any chances. The earth shook even more as the train approached. Couldn't she see we were right in the path of the oncoming train?

"Maria!" I shouted. "Maria, get out of the way." Her name sounded so strange on my tongue. I grabbed her hand and tried to wrestle her away from that spot. She laughed and did her best to make me stay. The steam engine was now dangerously close and I released my grip. I clambered across a few rails and turned back. There was Maria making the same signals with her arms as the little old man had done with the flags. And wonder of wonders, the engine slid effortlessly with clicking sounds onto the next set of rails. The passing engine sprayed her with a fine mist of steam and the black-faced white driver waved at her.

Totally drenched, she came to join me at the back door. "You should've stayed, Joseph," she said breathlessly. She brushed a few wet strands of hair from her face. "It really is good. Especially on a warm day like this."

I looked at her with amazement. That such a little girl, hardly six years old, could make a train switch tracks of her own will was magic beyond belief. She asked me to stay and wait for the engine to pass again so I could get my share of spray. I went to the front of the house and waited for Ma to return.

TOWN AND COUNTRY

WHEN MONA FINALLY DECIDED TO GO AND WORK IN THE CITY, Ma became very worried. For two whole days, only interrupted by sleep, Ma warned her about tricksters, robbers and killers stalking the streets. Each warning was followed by a story about a mishap that happened to a relative, dear friend or just somebody. I am sure the warnings terrified me more than my sister. They usually went like this: "Now be careful of those swanky-looking guys with the hard eyes. One of them offered to buy your Aunt Mieta's daughter a train ticket when there was a long line-up, and disappeared with her money. He said to her that he knew the guy at the ticket office and would get her ticket quicker. She missed her train and lost her job at the factory." As for the people Mona was going to work for, we just assumed they would be as good as my one aunt, who had worked for their parents for twenty-five years, said they were.

It all seems so very long ago, but it was only two years since we were at the small railway station to see Mona off. The train, with its electric lights and warmly dressed passengers, held a strange fascination for me. There was the beautiful deep-green upholstery contrasting sharply with the highly polished oak. A gleaming rail, on which were reflected the overhead lights and the passengers' movements, ran the entire length of the corridor. Only the travel-weary seemed at ease. Those who had just got on kept a shrill aloofness in finding a seat, confirming a reservation or saying goodbye for the umpteenth time.

Mona gave me a big hug. I was embarrassed by all this and suddenly didn't know what to do with my hands and feet. It seemed as if everybody was staring at us. Holding my hands behind my back, crossing one dusty bare foot on top of the other, I was immediately aware of our utter poverty. Ma said that I should have put on my other shirt, more for the benefit of the people surrounding us. We both knew the other shirt was kept strictly for church and Sunday school. And so I said nothing.

The engine let out a burst of steam and the guard blew his whistle for the last time. At the small Karoo station, the sounds were at once very loud but were then immediately lost in the darkness and the immensity of open space. With a noisy release of brakes, the train started into motion, marked by a series of clangs as each coach was pulled underway. The wheels closest to us were slow in moving and the acceleration was only shown in each successive set of wheels passing, until I could no longer see the wheels except for the swift passing of each coach. After the entire train had passed, there was nothing to see of it except the light spilling into the darkness and the sound of its movement—clickety-clack, clickety-clack.

At first Mona came home every end of the month. Each time she looked more beautiful than the last time. She always wore a new dress, but what I liked most was the warm smell of powder and perfume mixed with her own smell. Laden with parcels, she would arrive with something for each of us. There would be shoes, clothing and ornaments. Ma always complained that Mona brought her nothing but I know she handed over most of her pay.

Although my sister was not his own, I thought Pa was more proud of her than Ma was. I could see it in his looks when Mona was home and everybody's eyes on the farm were on her. Whenever we went grocery shopping on Saturday mornings at month-end and she talked too much with the older boys, Pa always called her away with a sharp, "Mona!" She then rejoined us, her face glowing from the recent attention. Pa made threatening noises and looked sternly in the boys' direction. Afterwards, on the back of the *baas*'s open truck, she seemed so out of place with the earthiness and smells of fellow farm workers. When she had to leave on Sunday evenings for the city, Pa was always busy puffing on his pipe in the vegetable patch. Removing a leaf here, a twig there, he occupied himself to shorten the embarrassment of saying goodbye.

While she was away, I thought she lived in a different world. It was a world inhabited by people called Madam and Master with their children Esmerelda and Jacques. They must have been very different from us and even from the white people who own this farm. From Mona's accounts, they sounded very clean, lived in a

big house and spoke English. Two times I heard English spoken at
the village store and both times it sounded so beautiful. The people
who spoke it were very white and handsome and drove nice big
cars. Of course I did not understand a word, but it sounded so
otherwordly, so musical, almost like soap bubbles floating to the
tune of music. I thought I must learn to speak the language to get as
rich as those people. Then again, perhaps one could only be born
into that kind of environment. But if my sister could leave this
place where my father and the other men had to work so hard just to
eat at least for four days out of the seven, then surely I could do the
same. I only had to work hard at school, my teacher said.

After six months, Mona no longer came home every
month-end. Instead she sent money by postal order which, of
course, made it difficult for Ma. Since Ma was not able to read or
write, she first asked me how much the paper was worth and then
went to the village store to make her cross, to pay for the new bed
and kitchen suite Mona bought on hire-purchase from the
catalogue. Pa said Mona had a man in the city, but Ma felt that
maybe she just had too much work to do at the white people's place
with all those parties and things always going on. To this my father
said nothing. Ma used to work in the city, too, until she had to come
back to the farm with Mona.

Sometimes at night, lying on my new bed in the kitchen, I could
hear them discussing Mona and me. Pa said maybe I should start
working on the farm next year when I turn thirteen. After all, we
couldn't be dependent on Mona's earnings forever. She was now
almost nineteen and hadn't had a serious affair yet. Of this he was
very proud. But then she might fall pregnant or get married and
who was going to pay the furniture bills? On his income he could
hardly afford to have food on the table everyday. Ma said he
shouldn't be so *swartgallig*—pessimistic—and have faith in his
daughter. Maybe with her assistance, I could get two or three years
of high school and then wouldn't have to work the rest of my life on
the farm. With those two or three years I could become a clerk with
a good job in the city. After all, he didn't want his only son to end
up the way he did? Pa's only security in this life was the
back-breaking work on the farm and us, his family.

With the extra money coming in, Ma sent me to the boarding
school in Graaff Reinet, a hundred miles away. I hated the school
and the town children with their stylish ways. All the time I was

there, I never made a single friend. On my fourteenth birthday I felt so lonesome I wanted to run away. Only the thought that Mona was paying for my education made me stay.

Two years went by and a letter arrived when I was home for school holidays. As usual, I read the letter for Ma. In it Mona said she was sorry for what she had done, but the Madam no longer "wants me around the place." Ma made me read it two times and then burst into tears.

"Yes Jan," she said, "you have to start on the farm now! Your sister has disappointed us and we have no way of keeping up with the boarding fees and such. Maybe if we tried, some relative can find you a job at a factory in the city."

Later, when Pa came home, she made me read the letter to him too. He immediately started swearing. "This comes from working in the city! I wonder if she knows who the father is." All this was very strange to me. Nowhere in the letter did it say anything about a pregnancy or a baby. It seemed Pa was more angry about the furniture payments that had to be made. The prospect of a baby didn't upset me. In fact I liked it. There would be the brand-new baby blankets, baby toys and even a new person in our family.

Waiting in the shade of a bluegum patch, I could feel the oppressive heat of the late afternoon sun. The station and the trains no longer held any attraction for me. The warm wind brought more dust than comfort. A torn, yellowed piece of newspaper was suddenly deposited in front of us. From my position on the railway bench, I tried to read the fine print without picking it up.

"Jan!"

"Yes, Ma."

"Just hand me that piece of paper."

I picked it up and gave it to her. She rolled it into a neat ball and threw it under the bench.

Soon the train pulled in. The white steam coming from the engine gave an illusion of coolness. That was all. Otherwise the magic was gone. Bleary-eyed passengers stared listlessly through the open windows. I mentioned to Ma that I wanted to help Mona with her parcels and anxiously got into the third-class carriage. The wood panelled compartments with the green upholstery seemed unbearably hot. There was dirt everywhere. Banana peels, papers and wrappers were strewn all over the floor. I finally spotted Mona waiting her turn to get off in the cramped corridor.

Now coming home after the letter, she looked very subdued. I immediately checked for telltale signs of pregnancy, but my sister just seemed a little plumper. She wore no lipstick and only her clothes set her apart as somebody special. She hugged me and I sensed a terrible sadness about her. I tried to find her eyes but she wouldn't look into mine. She also greeted my parents with downcast eyes. There were no presents for anybody; only two blue plastic suitcases which I gingerly placed on the back of the donkey cart. Pa had said even though Mona had shamed us, we had to get her from the station as she was our responsibility. Ma was very quiet while we were in the vicinity of the railway station. Once we were on the farm road, she started swearing to the high heavens.

The suitcases contrasted sharply with the roughness of the donkey cart. Feeling the pseudo-leather under my fingertips, I wondered what they contained. Perhaps just Mona's clothing and stuff. But then her clothing always held a mystery to me. By themselves, on the washing line, they were only clothes. Once on her, they seemed to come alive. It was almost as if a dress was an extension of herself when she wore it.

On the ride, Pa was very quiet. Only talking to Hester and Kammies occasionally (he never uses a whip on them), he seemed deaf to all the abuse Ma was pouring on Mona. My sister was very quiet too. Sobbing quietly behind the riding seat, she cringed when Ma's voice grew louder.

I wished I could comfort my sister, but this was adult business and I had no say in such matters. Maybe I could just touch her hand and give her some comfort. I stretched out my hand behind me and touched her knee. Mona flinched away. Turning around, I was embarrassed to the root of my toes. Her hands were covering her face. The moment of sympathy was lost in total misunderstanding. Maybe I could talk to her later when we got home.

Arriving at our two-roomed shack, I wondered what new sleeping arrangements would be made. My sister was a woman now. She could no longer sleep with me under the same blanket in the kitchen. I would have to sleep on the floor. Ma immediately ordered her to have a bath before she could set foot in the house. Somehow, Mona had to wash herself clean of sins before she could enter the shack she was born in. Ma took Mona's suitcases into the house and started busying herself with the pots and pans. My sister went to crouch at the back of the house. She tried to make herself into an invisible little ball. Occasionally she sobbed quietly while hiding her face in the crook of her arm. In the meantime, Pa started the outside fire and I hauled buckets of water from the communal tap. There were all-knowing looks from the older women while I waited my turn. They took their time in shutting the the tap and loading their buckets onto their heads.

Mona waited for darkness. Then she got up and went to have her bath. We used a forty-four gallon drum cut lengthwise and set at the side of the house, out of the neighbours' view. "Jan!" she called to me.

"Yes Mona?" What could she want from me now?

"Just come here for a minute please."

Afraid to see her, I peered around the corner of the house. She was completely submerged. Only the outlines of her hips showed a dull brown shape under the water. Slightly embarrassed, I raised my eyes to her face.

"Please bring me the soap, Jan."

There was something new in her look. Instead of shame or self-pity, I saw a new pride glowing in her eyes. Was this because of the child she was carrying? I couldn't tell. Running like a schoolboy at the teacher's request, I darted into the kitchen and grabbed the bar of Sunlight soap from the window-sill.

THE NEW MAN

IN MY NINTH YEAR HE CAME. WE NEVER SAW HIM ARRIVING, though. One morning he was just there, the young man of the twenty-odd summers with his laughing blue eyes and the blond hair of the *Hongkoiqua,* the smooth-haired ones, who walked as if he had no cares. With the early morning sun behind him, his body cast a long, thin shadow over the whitewashed farmhouse. Only when he turned to answer our greetings did I see that he was of average height. For a very brief instant, the sunlight gleamed and sparkled on his boots and coat buttons. Perhaps it was his military past which gave him his air of purpose. These were my first impressions of Jean du Plessis.

When he arrived on this farm, his presence held so much promise. In this land where the *Hongkoiqua* rule as absolute masters and our existence depends on their benevolence, he gave us a different view of life. Maybe he should have been a stronger man and perhaps then his compassion would not have been his weakness. But if he had been stronger, maybe there would have been no difference between him and the other white men.

There had been many other white men with blue eyes and blond hair who had come this way. Some worked for six months and others a year or so in the vineyards. Ultimately they always left for the interior. The promise of wealth inland was too strong an attraction, so they left this place for the gold fields and diamond mines. The temporary sojourn on this wine farm was only a chance to raise enough money for that journey inland. Most of them had arrived penniless at Cape Town.

These white men would, in their broken Dutch and attempts at the Khoikhoi language, speak of war and rumours of war. That seemed to be the sum total of their lives in countries called Prussia, Luxembourg, Flanders and so on. To me these places were merely names, but from the light in their eyes, I could see that to the *Hongkoiqua* they were places of much suffering and death. Until Jean du Plessis came, I never knew what white men thought; only what they remembered and what work needed to be done. But Jean took the time to explain that farm workers in his home country were no better off than us in South Africa. When I told him I always thought white men were bred in Europe to be bosses in my land, he said it wasn't so. "There are rich and poor everywhere," he answered, "but that is no reason for people to suffer. Things can be changed."

He himself didn't come here to be a boss. He came to work and was made a boss.

Sometimes the Dutch East India Company would send young white girls from an orphanage in Europe. They never lasted very long either. Indentured to become wives of the colonists, their job was to learn the elements of housekeeping. Jasmina, the cook, had the job of training these youngsters. She never got much training done, because at these times the old *baas* would always hang around the kitchen and wait for a chance to rape the girls. I suppose a second white woman, even a child of twelve, was too much for him to resist. Needless to say, it was always his wife, the old *nooi,* who chased the girls off the farm afterwards.

After a week of working under Jean, I started getting comfortable with his presence. I learnt he was a man of few words, not because he couldn't speak our tongue, but that this was his nature. Instead of overseeing our work, he'd more often join us in cutting and pruning the vines.

The *oubaas* didn't like this at all.

"Well, Jean," the *oubaas* said one day. "You sure have a knack for these pruning shears. Which part of France are you from again?"

"Alsace, Monsieur. My family, they lost all in the war."

"And how did you escape?"

"I, Monsieur, I just ran and walked until I came to the *mer* at Marseilles."

There was a moment's silence between them. I collected a bundle of cuttings and took it to the end of the row of vines. When I got back, the *oubaas* was just getting ready to leave.

"Life is hard, Jean, and you're a very good worker. But I want you to be firm with my workers. Be friendly, but be firm. A white man will not survive in this country if he doesn't show strength and character. You understand me?"

"*Oui*, Monsieur."

I suppose in any society where there is peace and justice, Jean would have had no problem adapting himself to fit the ways of the people. At peace with himself and those around him, he seemed content with merely being alive. Ours was a society of neither peace nor justice, and he should never have come here.

One day, after the second daily wine rations had been dished out, Jean followed us to the labourers' compound. From a few chimneys, thin wisps of blue-white smoke were already spiralling toward the pale blue heavens while a few women were still chopping kindling in preparation for supper. In an attempt at friendliness, small *baas* Jean started sharing his tobacco with the men scattered about the yard. I left the company of the men to do my chores but couldn't help overhearing part of a conversation between Piet and Willem.

"Why is this white man always hanging around us?" Piet asked.

"Don't you like his tobacco?" Willem replied.

"That's not the point. I can't look at the face of my *baas* for so long in the day."

"Well, the man seems honest enough. But you know the honky from overseas. They always start out this way. Soon enough he'll change his ways and know his place."

But things didn't change. After a month, we noticed Jean's eyes kept following Lena wherever she went.

My sister was not the most beautiful of women. At fifteen years of age, she was so angular and thin you could tie a shoestring around her waist. But in her walk and movement there was a catlike, easy grace which reflected an air of freedom. Everything she did had a musical quality to it. When picking potatoes, her long fingers would move swiftly from one potato to the other while her back remained bent, and she never raised her head until she had to move her feet. Then there was the liquid-smooth movement of foot, leg, thigh and hip to the next row. All this came as unconsciously as her breathing.

Of all the workers on this farm, the kitchen helpers seemed to think they had a monopoly on the white man's language. In the company of the white woman and her children for most of the day, they'd afterward in the labourers' compound mimic every accent and tone and think themselves better than other blacks. My sister Lena also used to work in the kitchen, but she never changed her ways. Although, like us, she spoke Afrikaans with the rhythm, idiom and accent of our own Khoikhoi language, her voice had a soft, melodious quality like a rippling brook in the forest. None of this Boer Afrikaans, affected by the kitchen help, would ever come from her mouth. Even when she cursed and swore, there was a sweet quality to her voice. Of course the men went crazy for her. Then she behaved as if none of them were good enough. I was often bribed with a lump of sugar, a bit of beef jerky or some toy just to carry messages to her.

Well, Jean wouldn't have had any difficulty in getting a pretty woman from his own race. At first he merely looked at Lena. Later he reserved the easiest work for her in the barn. Then he always went in with her to count crates, sweep the floor, or do one of the many small jobs nobody else had time for.

I once sneaked up on them. Through a crack in the woodwork, I saw Lena counting hessian bags and deftly piling them in neat bundles. Farther on my left, the small *baas* repaired some piece of machinery. Every now and then he'd take a peek in her direction. She seemed to ignore him completely. A few times he cleared his throat as if to say something, looked in her direction and, receiving no response, resumed his tinkering. I left the peephole feeling sorry for the shy man.

One evening I overheard Ma and Lena discussing him.

"Ma, I don't like the way this white man is looking at me."

"Yes, my child. Just stay out of his way and do your work."

"I am doing my work, Ma. But he's always sending me to the barn and then he follows me."

"Yes, my child."

"Ma, he's not like other men. What I mean to say is that he says nothing but just hangs around. And then there's Willem, Ma."

"Yes, my child."

"Ma, what I'm trying to say is that Willem has asked for homerights to come and visit and I don't know what the white man has in mind. I don't want a child from a white man, Ma. They all just up and leave you."

"Just leave it to me, Leentjie."

The following afternoon, I went with Ma to the small *baas*'s room in the *oubaas*'s backyard. Ma stopped a little distance from his door and sent me to call Jean. He emerged with a happy look on his face and gave me a farthing for my efforts. Ma was wringing her hands when we got to her.

"Small *baas*, I only want to speak *padlangs* straight. My child does not know how she has it with the small *baas*. It has now been a considerable time that my child has been so uneasy."

"I hear you, Toekoe."

"Small *baas*, my child is still very young and if things cannot improve, I will have to send her to another relative on some other farm."

He straightened his shoulders and took both of Ma's hands in his own. "I did not mean any harm, Toekoe. How can the child think such things of me? Why didn't she speak to me herself? She's such a sweet and kind-hearted person and I was only trying to be helpful. She seems a fragile person and I didn't want to overburden her. Please tell her that I'd like to speak to her myself."

I could almost see his mind at work. This occasion had given him the chance to say to Lena all the things he had so long carried inside himself. Besides, it wasn't as if he was forcing her into anything. Ma would be sending Lena to him. In parting, he went to get a pail of rice and some sugar from his room and gave it to Ma. She was pleased.

"Now you see what I have to put up with for you two?" she said to me on the way home. "I have to be both mother and father. Hopefully you'll appreciate it one day."

"Yes, Ma," I replied.

Whatever ill feeling she might have had against the white man was now absolved by the gifts. When Lena came home from work, Ma told her to return the empty pail and hear what *baas* Jean had to say.

Lena refused. "But Ma, surely Jonah can take it back? I don't want to talk to that man."

I immediately protested that I still had to feed the chickens. Seeing this man twice in one day was too much for me. He always gave me something and I had nothing with which to reciprocate. Once I took him two gold-spotted finch eggs and he angrily told me to replace them in the nest. I learnt then that he had a great reverence for life and also that, as a poor person, I could give him only my friendship. I refused to listen to Lena's excuses and went off to do my chores.

When I returned I found that she had gone after all. Later in the evening she returned. She was very quiet and answered Ma in a subdued voice.

"Did you see the white man?"

"Yes'm."

"What did he say?"

"Oh, nothing really."

"And what took you so long?"

"Oh he just wanted to talk."

Ma was getting ready for bed. "Well, I hope that has put an end to your fretting and worries. Goodnight."

"Night, Ma."

Afterward Lena sat at the kitchen table for a long time, drawing lines with her thumbnail in the open grain pine top.

In the weeks and months that followed, my sister grew plumper and stronger. There was a noticeable swelling in her stomach and the other girls started teasing her about "carrying a white man's child." At first she denied she had anything to do with small *baas* Jean. As her stomach became bigger, she told them it was none of their business.

Now there was meat in the house every day. Ma accepted the meat, flour, coffee and sugar gratefully from small *baas* Jean. To Lena she was alternately abusive and consoling. "How could you allow yourself this? My own child pregnant with the seed of the *Hongkoiqua*. The honky will flee like all the others."

"No, Ma," Lena pleaded. "The man promised he will marry me."

"Marry you? No way will he marry you. Just you mark my words."

In the evenings, she spread *buchu* powder over Lena's feet and in the old language prayed for a safe delivery.

Lunchtimes and evenings, my sister and her lover became inseparable. Sometimes I'd catch them sitting quietly side by side in the shade of an oak tree. Not a word would pass between them. Being in love was enough.

There was great joy in our house when the child was born. All the women came to see the blue-eyed child whose father had not deserted him. When finally Jean came, it took much prodding and insistence from Ma to get him to bury the afterbirth in the back yard as is the custom with our people. They don't have such customs with the *Hongkoiqua* but, since he stayed, Ma said he must learn to share the responsibility with the pleasure.

It was just before harvest, when the child was about one year old, that his father asked the *oubaas* for a special request. I remember the morning very well. The air was crisp and clean and a light frost covered every blade of grass in a silvery white sheet. If the frost came too early, a whole crop of grapes could be destroyed. Now that the grapes were already ripe, the frost merely increased the sugar content. This made the *oubaas* very happy. When he was happy, all of us were overjoyed.

On this morning small *baas* Jean asked the *oubaas* if Lena could move into his living quarters with him. He explained self-consciously that they had been going out for such a long time that they wanted nothing else but to be together. It sounded such a beautiful request that I stopped loading the wine wagon and watched him talking with much gesturing where the words failed to come.

Of course I had already seen this coming for a long time. It was almost as if he was part of our family now. Except on rare occasions, I hardly called him "small *baas*." He was more like an older brother to me and I called him by his first name. This upset quite a few people but he didn't care. I was his *"mon ami."* At home, Lena washed and mended his clothes like a married woman would. On Sundays he'd even eat over at our house.

Most of his free time was spent at our place playing with the child or telling Ma stories from the old country. At other times he'd tell us about the wonderful plans he had for Lena and his child. How he was going to build a house with many windows, a house which would be bigger than any of us had ever seen. There'd be separate bedrooms for him and Lena, special rooms for eating and dancing, and a parlour where she'd be able to receive her guests just like the rich people in his country. I wanted to ask him what a "parlour" was but Ma cut me short with a hard stare. Quite obviously she enjoyed hearing Jean speak as much as I did and wanted no interruptions. Lena, on the other hand, had no time for idle talk. She'd invariably be busy puttering around the kitchen and, if there wasn't any work to do inside the house, she'd keep herself busy in the garden. Once he mentioned wistfully that he'd like to show his child to his relatives overseas. However, he never once said how he was going to make the money for all these fanciful plans.

This question of their living together seemed such an innocent, small thing that I thought the *oubaas* would readily agree. After all, Jean was a model overseer. There were hardly any problems with any of the farm workers. All the work was done on time and there was nothing the old *baas* could complain about. His ferocious attack came as a total surprise.

"I've been watching you for the past year, Frenchman!" he shouted in his hoarse, wheezy little voice. "I've been watching you! All around people are talking about you and this *Hotnot meid.*"

"But, Monsieur..." Jean answered. He looked so embarrassed, he did not know what to do with his dexterous, capable hands. "Please, Monsieur."

"Don't Monsieur me!" the *oubaas* retorted. "And be quiet while I'm speaking!"

"*Oui*, Monsieur," Jean answered meekly. He clasped and unclasped his hands behind his back.

"Now listen to me. You're a good and honest worker." The *oubaas* suddenly became aware of my presence. Totally engrossed in this verbal assault, I stood as if rooted to the ground. I felt so much for Jean that it seemed as if the old *baas* were attacking me personally. He turned his old, grizzled face toward me. "Stop staring at me, Hotnot! Go get some work done!"

I turned my back on them, mumbled, "Yes, *baas*," and started unpacking the crates from the wine wagon.

"Like I said you're a good worker," the hoarse, wheezy little voice continued behind me. "But what you want to do now is totally against church rules. It's even against my own principles. You can have as many of the black bitches as you want, but I won't allow you to sink so low as to live with one of them. It's totally immoral!" He screamed, "Totally immoral! You hear me, Frenchman? Here you'll do as I say!"

"*Oui*, Monsieur," came the trembling reply.

"It's either that or you fuck off from my farm."

I wondered for a minute whether Jean was going to stand up to him. Give him some rude reply or even fight him. Jean was, after all, a white man. I wanted him to fight the *oubaas*. Either through words or by using his fists. How could he betray my sister by letting another man call her a black bitch?

The quick footfalls of Jean's shoes on the gravel made me glance over my shoulder. A feeling of utter contempt took hold of me. Instead of fighting it out, the man was running away from his problems.

Halfway to the farm gate Jean stopped in his tracks and turned around. A new resolve seemed to have taken hold of him while he approached the *oubaas* again. "Monsieur," he begged. "Will you let me stay on as an ordinary worker? I promise I will work harder than before."

Jean and Lena moved into a two-room structure in the compound. Lena did her best to keep the place neat and tidy. However, the flowers she planted were always trampled by jealous neighbours and once somebody defecated just outside her front door. In the fields, Jean worked harder than the rest of us. The new overseer was a brutal man and always taunted Jean about his "*Hotnot* wife." To all this Jean was deaf. He now had a wife and two children to care for, and with his reduced income he had a hard time feeding his family.

Although Jean was now regarded as less than a white man, we workers still had a measure of deference for him. Even in his reduced state we learnt from him that a man could forgo tobacco and wine so his children could eat a good meal. Besides, he never complained to anybody. I suppose he must have thought his condition was of his own choice, ultimately, and not to be blamed on anybody else. With such goodness, perhaps he should have been a missionary. Yet with all that suffering he still remained proud of his origins and his culture. In his free time I'd see him laboriously teaching his eldest blue-eyed daughter the language of the French people.

And one day it happened. His attempts at keeping a vegetable patch and a few chickens and sheep were destroyed when the *oubaas* came to tell him he had no right to raise anything on this farm without permission. The chickens and sheep were slaughtered and the meat distributed among the rest of us. The vegetables were dug up and fed to the *oubaas's* pigs. Ma felt too broken-hearted to return the meat to Lena and Jean. Instead she fed it to the dogs.

When finally he was reduced to a state of absolute dependence like the rest of us, the drinking started. The *oubaas* saw this and exploited it. Jean was given a double portion of wine in the morning and evening because he was "still a white man." Like most of the desperately poor, Jean became a bully. He beat up my sister after his drinking bouts. She'd tell Ma how he'd afterward possess her with the ferocity of a lion. Perhaps in his embraces he wanted to rid himself of his own weakness and pour it into Lena.

I was about eighteen years old when I couldn't stand his behaviour any longer.

"Jean du Plessis!" I confronted him one afternoon. "I'm sick and tired of you beating up my sister."

"Mind your own business," he answered. His breath stank of stale liquor. "I'll do as I please." He stared at me contemptuously through puffed-up, red-rimmed eyelids.

I tried to be conciliatory. "Don't you see that the way you're carrying on isn't doing anybody any good?"

"Tell your sister that. You go tell her to be a good wife and I'll change. She's the cause of all this!" He shrieked, "You're all ganging up against me. So just fuck off, I've got no time for you!" He made a wild lunge at me.

From a few doorways there were curious stares. I hated this encounter with the man. He was part of my family. Besides, at his age men on this farm do not behave like fools.

"Jean," I implored him. "I don't want to fight you. I just want to talk."

He was crying in his drunken fury. "All these years I've sacrificed for your sister and she hasn't given me an ounce of thanks. Not you, not she, not anybody! I could've been a rich man but she kept me in this bloody place."

I wasn't really angry now. I felt only a deep embarrassment. Before he could go any further and tell the whole world how he'd fed us in meagre times, I gave him two quick slaps across the face. A look of utter surprise showed in his eyes and he grabbed for a stick lying nearby. This time I gave him two solid punches in the jaw followed by a blow in the ribs. Then I beat him till I was tired.

I suppose that under any other circumstances I would have

been in serious trouble for beating up a white man. But nobody cared any more for this shell of a man. Not one of the workers went to report to the old *baas* that I was beating up his erstwhile overseer. A small crowd had gathered to watch the spectacle and from the teenaged boys came a few sniggers. I felt no sense of victory; only a deep and profound shame as he cringed before me in the dirt.

Lena struggled to get through the throng but I shoved her angrily away. What more did she want from this loathsome drunkard?

Another growl came from the broken figure. He shouted at me through broken teeth, "You're just a bully and a beater of old men!"

This time I could have killed him if Ma hadn't come in between us. I turned my back and walked away. Behind me sudden peals of raucous laughter broke the tension. Jean struggled to his feet and ran to escape the jeers from the onlookers. The next morning he was gone. Nobody could tell me where he'd gone or when he had left. I felt so much remorse afterward. How could I have beaten the man knowing full well that he was already a broken reed?

Two years after his departure, Jean du Plessis made a sudden reappearance. He came back wearing a flowing white robe. He looked a lot like Moses with his long hair and golden beard. I asked him what had brought him back, and he said he came to bring me Jesus.

FOR ONE POUND A DAY

AT THE HEAD OF THE COLUMN WALKS GROOTMA, GREAT mother, most revered member of the community and mother of Elizabeth, the union woman. Like most women her age, Grootma is almost as wide as she is tall. In addition, elephantiasis has left her with tree-trunk legs which make walking difficult, if not on some days impossible. The sun has been up for about half an hour and the column kicks up small clouds of dust while it moves along the dirt road. The fifteen women are of different heights and girth but in their white smocks they all resemble giant, animated peanuts waddling down the street.

Today, like every weekday morning, they are the first to leave for the day's work at the canning factory. Getting up when all was still dark outside, their movements in the gloom of candlelight were frantic. Very few people have clocks and the bus driver never waits for latecomers. Now, dressed in snow-white starched uniforms, they are on their way to meet the company bus at the entrance to the township. All of them are advanced in years, between the ages of fifty and sixty, and hold positions as supervisors. They have to be at work at 5:30 in the morning to make sure the machinery for peeling, cooking, canning and labelling are in order and readiness for hundreds of women workers starting at 7:00. Most important, they have to see the crates of fruit are set close to the sorting tables and conveyor belts.

Last night their union called for a strike to start today. However, the leadership was divided on the tactics. Elizabeth, the president, argued that people should stay at home for the entire week. The company is most vulnerable at this time of year and, with harvesting at a peak, will certainly meet the union's demand of one pound a day for every worker. Rachel, the union secretary, was of the opinion that people would be breaking the law by staying home. In her emotional speech, the scrawny white woman with her ever-present handbag and white gloves stressed that South African law allows people to strike, but on condition they report at their place of employment and only then refuse to work. Rachel's flowered, shapeless dress did nothing to enhance a bony, angular figure. To most of those present at the meeting, she resembled a schoolgirl in adult clothes with red lips and all. Perhaps that's why most of them felt her place in the union was purely to take minutes and not concern herself with strikes, freedom or national liberation. Her motion, that all workers report for work and refuse to obey orders, was thoroughly defeated.

Not a word passes between members of this column. Only Grootma walks with the bearing of one whose conscience is clear. The rest keep on making furtive glances to see if anybody is watching them from the houses on this street. They are, after all, breaking a strike and none of them wants to be called "sell-outs" in the community. The closed doors on fifty identical houses are mute witnesses to these strike breakers.

One door toward the end of the street suddenly opens. "People!" a familiar voice calls. "Don't you know that the union called for a strike today?"

The group comes to a stop.

Dressed in her nightdress and leaning across the bottom half of the Dutch door, Elizabeth calls, "Have you no respect for the union?" Receiving no reply, she continues. "You don't even have any respect for me. You just walk past my house knowing full well that you are hurting me." She steps outside to confront them a few paces away. "No . . . No . . . No. This is no way for members of the Fruit and Canning Union to behave." Still there is no response from the group. Elizabeth has made them feel so guilty, nobody knows what to say. "Cheenee! You make me ashamed to be your president. Then you always complain that the union does nothing for you." Fearing she's driving them too far from her, Elizabeth concludes with a plea: "Please stay home this one day."

Several doors open and occupants in states of undress lean out to get a proper earful.

Grootma is loath to confront her daughter on a day like this. However, she has to speak as all eyes are now focused on her. "But, my daughter," Grootma says, "Rachel told us that it is illegal to stay at home. You know very well that we can strike but we have to turn up at work. Who will pay the rent and buy food when there is no money coming in? The things you said last night were great words but much was said in anger. Those who agreed with you were equally angry, but they did not think of their starving children then. Better get dressed and come to work my child." Having said her piece, she starts walking followed by the rest, who are relieved they are at least leaving with dignity.

Watching them go, Elizabeth feels she has to make one more attempt. It is taboo for her to confront her mother in public, but she still has to say something. "And Mildred, Ann and Gerty! Why do you hide behind my mother and don't speak for yourselves?"

The words hit the entire group like a whiplash and, for the barest moment, Grootma falters in her shuffling gait. At the end of the street the company bus is waiting, emitting small puffs of blue-white smoke. The group now proceeds with grim determination and downcast eyes to escape Elizabeth. Once at the bus, they jostle each other trying to get on first.

With a rumbling and clatter of gears, the bus moves away. It leaves a large oil stain on the gravel road and a cloud of black smoke temporarily suspended in the air.

For Elizabeth, the struggle is not yet lost. There are still about four hundred women and a few men who will be getting ready for work. Well aware of the effect she has on men and her power over women, the tall black woman starts speaking to the curious onlookers. They are waiting to see what she is going to do next. She turns into her house and comes out again.

"My people, today is going to be our day!" Holding a one pound note aloft, she shouts, "The time for slave wages is gone! From today we will not work for anything less than one pound a day." Addressing herself first to a skinny old man in oil-stained coveralls, she asks, "Hendrik, do you want to see your children suffering all the time because you don't earn enough? And Mieta, like all of us women you do not work at the cannery because you like it but because you have to." In a louder voice she continues, walking the length of the street. "It is time the company realizes that it cannot go on getting rich while we stay poor! Who drive the biggest cars, have the biggest houses and wear the best clothes? I tell you, it is the white people!"

Not a single door is shut. Instead, more doors are opened as people wake to her thundering voice.

In her agitation, Elizabeth forgets she is wearing only a nightdress. Her garment, like most, is not designed to conceal but to highlight her body. The early morning sun cuts through the flimsiness of her covering and etches her every contour and movement in stark relief. She suddenly becomes aware of her near nakedness. Crossing her arms to cover her exposed bosom, she can do nothing to conceal the panty lines on her ample buttocks. She is embarrassed; her speech falters while women watch her mouth and men devour her body. From one of the doors a woman sends a little girl of seven or eight with a man's raincoat. Elizabeth hugs the child, smiles and winks at the mother, and puts on the coat.

On their way to work, people from the side streets have started congregating about her. While most are on foot, a few listeners lean across the handlebars of their bicycles to listen intently to this woman. Those on the main road to town notice the commotion in Barbarossa Street and, discovering what it is, stay. Some just listen for a while and then leave quietly, clutching their brown paper lunch bags.

"I tell you people," Elizabeth says, "this is not only something that affects us at the canning company. Those of you who work for the textiles, builders, bakeries and winemakers must stand with us today because there is no difference between the white bosses. Each and every one of them gets rich on our labour."

Soon the crowd swells to over a thousand souls and it is no longer necessary for Elizabeth to run up and down addressing households. A chair is brought to make her visible to all listeners. In the crowd, lunch bags are shifted from one hand to the other. Some people, having given up the idea of going to work, are already munching sandwiches. By ten o'clock the crowd has not abated. A police van arrives but, unable to penetrate the dense mass of humanity, the policemen cannot get at the speaker. Standing on the roof of their vehicle, the policemen view her through binoculars. A pile of white cardboard sheets materializes from somewhere and a writer, armed with a felt marker, writes slogans as they are shouted to him from various points. Some of them read:

TODAY IS OUR DAY.
WORKERS UNITE FOR A FREE SOUTH AFRICA.
WE STRIKE FOR ONE POUND A DAY.

Elizabeth doesn't want the people to leave this spot right now. New strategies have to be planned to keep them together. She withdraws to her two-room house and leaves other women to circulate a hastily drawn petition. This is addressed to "ALL Bosses in Paarl" and demands a minimum of one pound a day for all workers irrespective of race, colour or creed. Then she sends one of her daughters to fetch Oom Barend, a renowned preacher and funeral prayer. A few minutes later, a dishevelled old man arrives in her bedroom.

"Oom Barend, we want God to be on our side today," Elizabeth says urgently. "Please come with me and speak to the people about how Israel was suffering."

"But I'm not dressed for it," he protests.

"God says, 'Come as you are,'" she says firmly. "These people are not dressed for church either."

"But I'm not political, Lizzie, you know that yourself."

"Oom Barend, I'm not asking you to say anything political. Just preach to the people about Israel."

"Oh, well, just give me a Bible then."

She does as he asks. Without another word, clutching the Bible for reassurance, he leaves the bedroom like a man with a mission. Elizabeth follows respectfully behind.

Outside, standing on a few packing crates rigged up for a platform, he starts the crowd off with, "Onward Christian Soldiers." The mood is set. After they sing the hymn three times, he raises his hands for silence and then reads from the Book of Exodus of how Israel suffered under Pharaoh. Oom Barend is overcoming his earlier unease. He is used to organized prayer groups in churches and houses where the proper atmosphere is created by Sunday best and the pious looks of fellow believers. He has never seen most of these people before him at a prayer meeting or church service. He also realizes that with his unshaved jowls, shoes without socks and pyjama top tucked in his pants, he does not look his normal preacher self. But he is going to give this meeting his best if it's the last thing he does:

"Beloved sisters and brothers, we have heard of the hardships suffered by the people of Israel. And as in Israel's time, our God is alive and sees the suffering of His people. He will only allow His people to bear the yoke for so long and then enough will be enough. God gave Israel a Moses to lead them. Likewise, God is giving you Elizabeth today."

A tumultuous roar comes up from the crowd. The roar is interspersed by piercing whistles. Thinking for a minute that the applause is for him, he starts telling them about his own experiences. "The sufferings of Israel were no different from my own suffering. For sixty years these two hands have worked. From early dawn until late at night. And what do I have to show for it today? Nothing! I tell you! Nothing! The white man has grown fat and rich while I remain as poor as the day I was born."

At this point, various people interject with loud Amens to punctuate the truth of his words. A few hecklers add, "Praise the Lord," and, "Alleluiah," but they are quickly silenced by a malevolent stare or a painful prod in the ribs from other listeners. Somewhere in a corner, a fist fight has begun. Noticing this, Oom Barend breaks off in the middle of his speech, holds up his hands for silence, and starts wading through the crowd toward the fighters. When he gets to them he shouts, "You stupid criminals! Why do you fight while God's word is spoken?" Taken totally unawares, they break up and stare uncomprehendingly at the old man. "If you are too stupid to listen to me, then leave this meeting. Leave us and go work for the Boers."

After what has been said about the whites, nobody in his right mind wants to be seen working today. Embarrassed, the two contestants drop their fists and lower their heads in shame.

"Now shake hands," Oom Barend commands. Obediently they comply and the old man turns his back on them. Amid much rejoicing he slowly makes his way back to the platform, where a beaming Elizabeth awaits him.

A new contingent of police arrives. Starting on the periphery, the policemen tell individuals that this is Monday and not a day for prayer. People should be at work instead of listening to rabble-rousers and false prophets. There are the few who are easily intimidated but, rather than obey the police, they merely shift to another spot in this sea of humanity. The majority stand their ground and some people sternly ask the policemen to be quiet as Oom Barend is about to pray.

"Almighty Father, today we have said many things in your name. Many things, Lord, because the needs of our people are vast. Deprived of a birthright in the land of our birth, we have become mere chattels to the white man. We do not ask for much, Lord. Only that our needs are met. That men and women should earn a wage proportionate to their needs and labour. That no one should die because there was no money to pay for the doctor. That we can share in the bounty of Thy earth and that this not be the exclusive right of a few. Grant us therefore, faithful Lord, the opportunity to prove our cause as just and right and, like the tribe of Israel, you will not send us away empty."

He finishes this appeal with the Lord's prayer, in which everybody joins. He concludes with a loud "Amen," repeated by the crowd.

The police, as if on cue, start lashing out with rubber truncheons and wooden sticks. A few men and women immediately converge around Oom Barend and Elizabeth. As if the action has been rehearsed many times before, they crowd the two leaders into the first available house and shut the door firmly behind them. Once they are inside, a woman checks the back yard for safety. Finding the yard empty, she beckons everybody to follow into the deserted lane behind.

Among the rest of the crowd there is immediate pandemonium. The old and infirm are trampled underfoot. Those who rested on a bicycle find a foot caught in the spokes or somewhere in the frame. Scattering like stampeded animals, the people flee sticks that hit at women's breasts, thighs and buttocks as well as men's heads. The ones who fall receive no mercy from the police. In fact, for a while the police concentrate on the wounded and fallen until the onlookers are shocked into helping their stricken comrades. Then it becomes a battle between stone throwers and the police. This brief respite gives the opportunity for the wounded to be pushed, pulled or dragged to the nearest doorway.

By ten o'clock the supervisors at the cannery have grown desperate for the arrival of their workers. Crates of apricots, peaches, grapes and pears are stacked ten cases high while the machines hum softly in readiness. Today, however, not a single pear will be peeled.

The managing director has been on the phone all morning telling the police commander to force the workers to work. By noon he gives up when he gets a report of the riot. In frustration, he runs down to the factory floor and shouts at the supervisors: "You useless bunch are all responsible for this! Can't you bloody well control your workers?" Receiving no reply, he starts switching off all the machines and overhead lights. "If these bastards don't show up for work tomorrow," he says, "everyone of you black bitches will be fired!"

"It's Lizzie, Baas," a voice pleads in the semigloom where some of the supervisors are gathered, whispering to each other.

"Don't Lizzie me! If I ever get my two hands on her she'll wish she'd never been born. What she needs is a decent fuck to straighten her out. And stop staring at me! Get the hell out of here!"

Grootma leaves last. An angry scowl is on her face.

Afterward, he phones the farmers and asks them to stop sending consignments of fruit. He is in no position to handle it. The entire white clerical staff is given the day off to arm themselves for civil defence. The riot is threatening to spill over into the white section of town. In the vineyards and orchards of the Boland, the farm workers are suddenly given a new and unprecedented order. Normally they are cursed and whipped into greater productivity; now they are told to stop for the entire day. What is picked is moved to the barn for temporary safekeeping. Of course, they will have to make do with less money at the end of the week, but it is not for them to question why. The *baas* has his reasons.

In the quiet white suburb of trimmed hedges, gravel sidewalks and dogs barking discreetly, Rachel is upset. Her class and politics, however, prevent her from sharing the anxiety with Maisie, her servant. Sitting at her husband's desk, Rachel avoids looking at his gilt-framed academic photograph. She concentrates on the gardener meticulously trimming a rose bush in the vast expanse of her green lawns.

Maisie has been giving her all kinds of news brought to the back door by the grocery delivery boy, the newspaper boy and the postman. The postman still has to make his second round but the news thus far has not been encouraging. Earlier, she heard that the army was patrolling the streets in the township. Later, that twenty people have been fatally shot. So far no reports about Elizabeth. Of course this is not the way Rachel wanted the strike to go. What she wanted was a sit-down strike at the plant, where police violence would be minimized and the confrontation directly aimed at management. There would be greater bargaining power if the workers could destroy the capitalist means of production.

However, she has to deal with a fait accompli and work with the means at her disposal.

She calls the editor of the English daily to check if the event was covered. Yes, tomorrow's edition will have full front-page coverage highlighting police brutality. Then she phones a few sympathetic lawyers to ensure legal defence is available for all arrested. She isn't sure where the money will come from to pay the lawyers, but at least they give her assurances.

About four in the afternoon, a dirty black urchin with a runny nose appears at the kitchen door. "*Molo*, Sisi," he calls through the fly screen.

Maisie breaks off from washing the dishes and recognizes him as Elizabeth's fourth born. "*Ufuna' ntoni mntan' mi?*" she asks. She opens the door to let him in.

"My mother, she says I must give the message to the Missus that she is fine," he says. He stops to stare about at all the fixtures in the kitchen.

"Is that all?" Maisie asks. She wipes his nose with a piece of paper towel.

"No, Sisi. My mother, she also said to say that *amabhulu* are breaking down people's doors looking for her." Without asking where his mother exactly is, Maisie sends him away with a thick slice of bread spread with peanut butter and jam. Then she goes to Rachel's study to give her the news.

Calling a close lawyer friend, Rachel checks what possible charges could be laid against Elizabeth, her comrade. The list he rattles off is quite long, but what sticks in her mind are the possibilities of economic sabotage and incitement to revolt. Each carries a minimum sentence of twenty years in prison.

"Mind you," the lawyer says, "she does have a chance—a slim chance, but it's nevertheless a possibility."

"What is it?" she asks, trying to sound calm.

"I'd call it a possible technicality at this stage. I mean if she were to plead not guilty to any of the possible charges because she was moved by the spirit to conduct a religious gathering, which was broken up by the police."

"That's if she ever gets as far as the law courts, Barry."

"Now what exactly do you mean?"

"There's been so many deaths in detention lately—this one hanged with a shoestring, that one slipped on a bar of soap—I can't imagine what they'll do to Elizabeth if she allows herself to be arrested." On the other end the lawyer is beginning to sound harassed. "Rachel, please try to remember that I'm an officer of the court. I can't very well counsel you contrary to my standing. I just can't tell someone to run away from the police."

"It's okay, Barry," she says firmly. "Thank you very much."

"I hope you understand. There's only so much I can do."

"I understand perfectly. Goodbye."

After she sets the phone down, she sits quietly for a minute or two. Her duty is to protect the leadership at all costs. What she has to do will be without Elizabeth's consultation. Speaking to her now is completely out of the question. If and when Rachel contacts Elizabeth, it will only be to tell her where and when an escape vehicle will be available. Besides being a trade unionist, Rachel is also a member of the banned Communist Party of South Africa. Within her cell are available some resources which can only be drawn upon in absolute emergencies. She feels this is such a time.

Taking a piece of paper from her desk drawer, she writes a brief note for the pharmacist three blocks away: "A packet of Aspro for Mrs. O, please." She seals the note in an envelope. Folding the envelope once, she inserts a one pound bill in the crease. This she gives to Maisie with instructions to give it to Mr. Waterman only, as she is suffering such terrible pains at her time of month.

At the pharmacy, Waterman reads the note carefully, gives Maisie a small packet of candy in an impressive looking carton and returns the one pound note. "Please ask the Missus to use this," he says. "If it works well, I will charge her the next time." Afterward, in the privacy of his office, he makes quick calls to two other cell members.

The next day people talk about having seen two very old white women driving through the township and giving black power salutes. Later still, the story grows. There were actually four old white women handing out guns to the rioters.

Three days have passed since Elizabeth spoke on that fateful morning. Nobody seems to know where she is. As for her five children, only the five-month-old baby still seems upset. However, he is in good hands. A mother who lost her own infant a week ago has started nursing him. Oom Barend says he is still waiting for the police to come for him. Dressed in his Sunday best, his Bible at hand, he has been waiting all day to be arrested so he can bring comfort to those in prison.

Grootma resigned from the Fruit and Canning Company yesterday. She says she cannot go on working for a white man who calls her a black bitch in her old age. Instead, with some help from a few women, she has started a day care for working mothers.

The canning factory passed out leaflets today which say the company will pay workers two pounds a day if they will start tomorrow. This, of course, will anger other employers in town.

THE BONUS DEAL

I HATE THIS CONSTANT BICKERING. IF IT'S NOT OVER MONEY, then it's over the smallness of this township house which has only a kitchen, living-room, and one bedroom. At their age I would have thought my parents would grow old quietly. There's nothing they can do about being poor now, but at least they should arrive at some inner resolve to accept each other because they're far too old to change. Last December Pa turned sixty, still too young for a government pension the social worker said. Besides, he still had a few small gardening jobs with some older white women in town. "Once you have no income, Attie," she promised, "I'll see if I can get you a disability allowance. It all depends on the people at Pretoria."

Mamma isn't all that young either. After years of working as a seasonal domestic, her legs are giving her a lot of problems. She says it's from having had to scrub and polish the white women's floors on her knees for most of her life. Even though we only live in a three-room structure now, she still keeps the place spotless and shining.

Pa lazes around all day sucking on his pipe and muttering to himself. Mamma, in turn, follows him all over the house. She straightens cushions on the couch, dusts for fingermarks and picks up bits of tobacco. He doesn't like Mamma's obsession with keeping the place tidy. "Wiesie, this is not a furniture store," he says. "It's a house." To this she pays no attention. Mamma says she has to keep herself busy; otherwise she'll die of boredom.

Before we got this place in town, we used to live in a very big old house on a wine farm. In fact, I was born on that farm. The house must have been centuries old. Perhaps it was built by the first Dutch settlers who came to this country hundreds of years ago. The whitewashed walls were three feet thick in most places. Overhead the beams were made of rough-hewn logs and the roof was covered with black straw. At night I could hear the mice playing in the rafters and, on looking up, would get dust in my eyes. Of course there was no inside plumbing. We also had to use a communual toilet. Now we have electricity and running water but there's hardly any room to sleep. Most of the time I have to wait for visitors to leave before I can make my bed on the kitchen floor. I still miss the cloying smoky fragrance of an extinguished candle before falling asleep, but sometimes the mere thought reminds me of bed bugs crawling out of the wall under cover of darkness. Some Saturday nights when Mamma baked a batch of cookies, she would let me stay up late with her. Sitting in the glow of the candle, I watched her kneading and rolling the dough into a fine white sheet. Sometimes I would get a few scorched cookies to nibble on. What I liked most, though, was when my older brothers and sisters came home late from a dance or party. Then they would quietly slip me a chocolate or some candy which I would save for eating later in bed.

From time to time I wish my older brothers and sisters were still with us. As grown-up men and women they might know how to put an end to the squabbles here. On the other hand, with so little room in this place, I wonder how we could all live here. Perhaps it's best they're raising their families on their own.

Things were not always good on that wine farm. Most of the time Pa would come home drunk from work and then there was a fight over food because there wasn't enough or because Mamma had cooked something he didn't particularly like. I hated those times. There was nothing we children could do to stop the beating and screaming. When my father beat her, she screamed and ran from room to room in trying to escape the blows. All the while this brute of a man chased after her and shouted, "Stop screaming! Shut your mouth!" Once I tried to protect Mamma from the blows, and he started flailing me with his army issue belt. Everybody knew my six-foot-tall father was the strongest worker on the farm, so none of the neighbours interfered when there was trouble in our household. Besides, my father was also insanely jealous. I'd seen him beat up another man just because he stared too long at my mother.

At other times he was so kind and helpful when Mamma was sick that he even stayed home to do the cooking and cleaning. But then he would always be frustrated and angry when, because he'd lost a few work days, he brought less money home on the next payday. Then all the kindness he'd shown would disappear and he was his angry, drunken self again. And Mamma, who had just got up from a sick bed, would get sick all over again.

At the age of ten I got so tired of all this that I ran away to the nearest town. I knew I would be in serious trouble for leaving the farm but I couldn't stand it anymore. For a whole week I lived on the streets, ate from garbage cans and wondered at night how my mother was doing. After I was caught and taken back by the police, the farmer, according to custom and law, gave my father two choices. Either I was going to be punished by the two policemen who had brought me home, or my father could give me a personal whipping in their presence. While the farmer spoke, the two policemen stood flexing their arms. Obviously they were quite keen to do the whipping themselves. Then, from the back of the police van, one of them got hold of two vicious-looking leather whips while the other one ripped my shirt off my back.

My father pleaded with the farmer, whom we all addressed as Baas as if our lives depended on it. "No, Baas," my father said. "Baas knows that I have never had any dealings with the law. Please, Baas, don't let him fall into the hands of the law." Didn't my father see there was no difference between the punishment meted out by officials and that administered by this farmer? That the same laws which allowed this white farmer to have me beaten like some animal he owned also gave the policemen the right to use their whips on me? To me there was no justice in any of the punishment. My father should have been the one to be flogged. He was the cause of all this. If he had a heart, he would have asked for total mercy. He should have told them he was to be blamed. Instead he insisted on flogging me himself.

I then pleaded and begged the *baas*. I said it wasn't through my own doing that I had ran away; that I couldn't stand the violence anymore.

This powerful man, who had our present and our future in his hands, started quoting from the Bible. "Honour your father and your mother," he said while biting on the stem of his pipe. When he finished his piece from the commandments, he dismissed the policemen: "Well, constables, thank you very much for bringing the little *Hotnot* home. You can go now."

"But Meneer," one of them protested, "are you sending us away without having finished our tasks? The law says —"

"The law be damned!" the farmer shouted. "Here on my farm I'm the boss. So just get off my property."

In their anger and frustration they raced from the farm as if the devil were chasing them.

Then, in the cool gloom of the barn, amid the fragrance of dried apricots, peaches and raisins, I was tied over a wagon wheel by Pa and one of the other workmen. The *baas* stood waiting to light his pipe. Perhaps the custom had its roots in a time when slave owners didn't have watches by which to time their floggings. Now, for as long as it took the *baas* to finish smoking a pipeful of tobacco, that's how long the whipping should last. I've heard of men given "four pipefuls" in the old days, but they couldn't have lived afterward. He struck a match and I felt the tip of the whip biting the flesh on my waist. Soon the pain became so unbearable that I lost consciousness and all was black before me. When I woke, Mamma was busy dressing the wounds on my back with *buchu* powder and cobwebs. She said the old medicine was best but I knew there was no money for a doctor.

In the days that followed, my father behaved very strangely. He came home from the vineyards as drunk as usual and, when he thought nobody was looking, he rushed to the outside toilet and tried to vomit all the wine he'd drunk. I suppose there wasn't much he could do about his enforced daily ration of wine. If he'd refused it outright, I'm sure the baas would have had him flogged for insubordination. So he drank his wine like a humble farm-hand, an obedient *Boerjong*, in the farmer's presence while something inside made him want to throw it all up afterward.

One evening, when he was making for the toilet again, Mamma was waiting for him. "Attie, you can't go on vomiting your guts out," she said. "Why don't you tell the Boer that you can't keep his rotten wine inside?"

Pa looked at her confusedly and stepped into the communal toilet. Over his shoulder he shouted, "Don't be stupid, woman! You want us to be chased from here like dogs? I'm doing this to be a better man." He bent his head, kicked the door shut and started vomiting.

The next day Mamma told us she was going to see the farmer about Pa's illness. She said she was going to see if she couldn't get the *baas* to give Pa less wine. Maybe if he only got to drink once a week his health would improve. Of course she couldn't go and tell him Pa's sickness and all our troubles were because of the twice daily ration of wine. But if she said Pa wasn't strong enough to drink everyday, maybe the *baas* would see her point. That evening, for the first time ever, my father came home not smelling of liquor. He was even playfully angry with Mamma and told her she was to be blamed if he ever died of thirst.

Although the other men started calling him "the weekend drunkard" behind his back, Pa was totally unconcerned. Gone were the days when he would come home staggering all over the place, crash into the furniture and curse everybody in sight. Now he always brought a little something home for Mamma or us in the evenings. If it was not a bunch of flowers he'd pilfered from the Boer's garden, then there would be an odd-shaped stone or carved animal for one of us. Sometimes, late at night, he stared into the flames of the stove and reminisced with Mamma about their courting days. How beautiful she had once looked in a particular dress when he had come to ask her father for *huisreg*, visiting rights. The time he had thought he was going to lose her to a handsome young worker from a neighbouring farm. There were many things he talked about but Mamma would say very little. Only occasionally would she correct him about a detail here and there. Otherwise she simply let his flow of words wash over her and she smiled with a warm glow.

Soon there was enough good food on the table everyday. On Saturday afternoons, my father would still get drunk with his best buddies while playing a long drawn-out card game of *Klaberjast* behind the house. There were occasional fist fights, but on the whole the men made up soon afterwards and resumed their drinking. By sundown he cleared the kitchen table of cards, packed away the empty wine bottles and told his friends he was getting himself ready for the Sabbath. He never did go to church on Sundays. Instead he busied himself around the yard and listened to the morning church services on the radio.

There was even a change in Mamma. Anytime of the week she would surprise us with fresh-baked cookies. Most of all, I marvelled at the worry lines disappearing from her careworn face.

Once, though, I caught her quietly sobbing in front of the stove.

"Why are you crying, Mamma?" I asked while I felt my insides heating up. "Is something the matter?" I suddenly wondered what secret evil deeds my father was committing.

"No," she answered, drying her eyes on her apron. "It's just that I'm so happy. Everybody's working. You are getting ready for high school. Why couldn't things be this good all the time?" And then she hugged me against her tightly, which made me so uncomfortable that my anger at my father disappeared into nothingness. Maybe she sensed the confusion within me, because she suddenly released me from her grip with orders to haul water and chop kindling on the double. I ran from her and felt so good that I almost cried myself.

Sometimes my father took me for long walks in the farmer's vineyard. In the spring he would show me the vines he'd planted with his own two hands twenty or thirty years before. I'd never really thought much of it since everybody else's father had probably had a hand in planting, pruning and harvesting some part of the vast vineyard. During summer there were many experiments with new grapes and new vines. Although we children never got to taste any of the new wines, we did occasionally get to eat grapes that tasted like pineapple, strawberries or even pears. One time I even crunched grapes that had the mustiness of chocolate.

With all this new money coming in, ours became the best furnished house on the farm. We had old Dutch furniture in the living-room and a paraffin fridge in the kitchen. I no longer had to wait for Christmas to get a new pair of shoes. Although Pa had said the *baas* didn't want any educated Coloureds on his farm, Mamma started to insist that at least I, the last born, become something else than a farm labourer.

I'll never forget that first day at high school. In my brand-new school uniform and shoes polished to a "Nugget shine," I was the pride and envy of the whole farm. Never before in living memory had a child from this farm gone on to high school. Just before I left, my older sister sprinkled a bit of cologne on me "to make you smell good for the town girls." I hated this and ran, embarrassed, down the farm road to wait for the school bus.

The next day before the first cock had crowed, the farmer was at our door. "Pack up your things and leave, Attie!" He shouted this at my father through the open door. "I've been bending over backwards to give you a weekly wine ration but this time you've gone too far!" Half-dressed in his underwear, my father cringed at this early onslaught. "Besides, you *bleddie* Hotnots have grown too rich for this farm."

"But Baas," Pa pleaded. "Can't Baas just give the little one a chance to get some education?"

Mamma tried to add her voice to the protest, but the Boer just silenced her with a loud shout. "No! Not a word more from either of you. If you're not off the farm by ten o'clock, I'll get the workers to throw you off!" He left the yard in a huff.

That day I didn't go to school. Instead, I helped Mamma pack all the smaller things while my older brothers and sisters loaded the furniture. Mamma was tearful when we left and quickly walked around the empty house. She spent an awfully long time praying in their empty bedroom until Pa had to shout at her to get into the removal truck. After months of living in the back yards of relatives, we finally secured this three-room council house.

One day Mamma spotted the farmer's red and green truck outside our door. "Now look who's here," she said. "Go see what the white man wants, my child."

I didn't feel like talking to him but went outside anyway. Halfway to the truck I decided there was no way I was going to call him "Baas."

"Mamma wants to know what you want," I inquired in an even monotone. I stared him in the eye.

Surprised at my insolence, his face turned red and he answered sheepishly. "Can you please ask your father to come and see me? I want to talk to him."

I ran back into the house with a good feeling. No white man had ever said "please" to me.

Pa wanted to put his jacket on before meeting his former lord and master. Mamma would have none of this. "Go out in your shirtsleeves," she told him. "We're no longer his servants. We're free people."

Mamma and I watched the two of them through the kitchen window. The white man got out from the truck and, in an attempt at friendliness, offered Pa his tobacco pouch. Pa politely refused and the man pocketed his pouch. After a few moments of furtively looking in our direction, the farmer said something and the two of them got into the truck and drove off.

Near sunset they returned. Pa came running into the house. "Wiesie! Wiesie! Something wonderful has happened! Our heads are through!"

She left her darning in the bedroom and came to see him in the kitchen. "What are you talking about, old man?"

Pa was beside himself with glee. "I told you our heads are through!" he shouted again. "I got my job back on the farm."

"Yes?" Mamma answered, nonplussed. "And what about Andrew's education? Can he still go to school?"

With all this moving around I hadn't been to school at all and had given up any idea of going back.

"No problem," Pa said. "The *baas* says everybody needs schooling in this day and age. And that's not all. I even got a bonus from the co-operative for the thirty years work I did on the farm!"

"Bonus money?" she asked disbelievingly. "Since when do farm workers get bonus money?"

He didn't like the way Mamma asked him about this. "What do you want to know about the money?" he demanded.

I feared he was going to fight her again so I went to sit in the living-room. From there I could see everything without getting hurt myself.

"Nothing really," she replied. "Do you think the Boer gave you the whole amount due to you?" She asked this quietly while filling the kettle for coffee at the kitchen sink.

"That's none of your business, Wiesie!" he said, suddenly exasperated. "This is my money and the *baas* said I must keep it for my old age. He was even so kind that he went to the bank and cashed the slip for me."

"What slip was this, Pa?" Mamma wanted to know. For a few years in her youth, she had worked as a seasonal domestic for rich white people in the city. Perhaps through them she had got to know a fair bit about banks and cheques. "Who sent you this slip? I never saw any slip around the house here." She rested her hip on the edge of the kitchen table and waited for his reply.

"Now there you go again," he said, staring out of the window. "All these questions and questions. You're never satisfied with anything you get." He rummaged through his pockets for his pipe before continuing. "As I've explained before, the money is from the Co-operative Wine Growers Association. The *baas* told me it is not for future work but a bonus to all farm workers with services of twenty years and more."

Mamma abruptly turned away from him and started stirring a

pot of stew. Facing him again, she said, "But why didn't you let me see the cheque first, old man? You know I can read and write, so why didn't you let me see it first? Maybe the *baas* has tricked you." She returned to the sink and, leaving him to think her words over, studiously rinsed a cup under the running tap.

I could see Pa felt himself completely ignored. Mamma has this way of shutting somebody completely out of her awareness. He made as if to speak, reached for his tobacco pouch and started filling his pipe. Between clouds of smoke he started again. "It is such a big amount of money that I really wanted to keep it a surprise for you."

"A surprise for when?" she asked over her shoulder.

"I thought we might need it for an emergency, like death or a confirmation for one of the children or something."

"And how much money was it?" she asked.

"It's so much money, Ma, that you've never seen in your whole life." After sucking on his pipe for a minute, he continued. "I've never seen so much money in my whole entire life."

"How much, I ask you." She turned to face him again.

"I counted three times and it came to five hundred Rand." He said this in an urgent whisper, as if he wanted to keep this knowledge from the very walls.

"Well sure," she continued, calmly, as if the amount held no special significance for her. "It is a fair amount of money, but do you know whether you got the whole amount?"

"What whole amount is this?" he asked. The beginning of anger and alarm crept into his voice.

"No, rather you tell me the whole story." She made herself comfortable on the other side of the table. "Like how did you get hold of this cheque that the *baas* went to cash for you. Just tell me the whole story and then we'll know whether we've been done in by somebody."

"In any case," Pa began, "he comes to me and says to me that the co-operative has started this thing of giving the farm workers a bonus."

"Why not a pension instead?"

"Don't interfere now! I'm telling my story, woman!"

"Then tell your goddamn story and get it done and over with."

Whenever Pa told a story, it seemed to me he used the grammatical rules from another language. Never did he use the past tense of daily speech. The story was told as if it were happening right there and then with the telling. Maybe this form of storytelling comes from the Khoikhoi language my ancestors used to speak. Mamma once told me both her grandparents could speak that language but as children she and Pa were forbidden to use it on the farm.

"So, the *baas* says to me that he has a surprise for me. I ask him, 'What is the surprise, Baas?' He shows me this piece of paper with many numbers written on it. Then he says for me to follow him to the office. So I walk behind him to the office and he says for me to come inside. I have never been in the office in my whole life and now I see all the important documents, books and papers and beautiful furniture. On the walls there are heads of lions, gnu and other animals, too many to mention."

"And you have never been to that room before?" she asked. She got up to pour some coffee.

"No, Ma. It was the very first time in my life, otherwise I would've told you so before. Not so?"

"Yes," she said, stirring sugar in the cups.

"So then the *baas* looks at me strangely and he says, 'Have you ever had any schooling in your whole life, Attie?' And I tell him, 'No, my *baas*. Except for that one year when I was about seven, I had no schooling. Otherwise I cannot even write my name,' I tell him. 'Well then, touch this pen, so that I can make a cross for you,' he says."

"You didn't even think of me at that time," Mamma asked. "That maybe I should read the slip first before he made the cross for you?"

Pa was almost crying now. He got up from the table and stared at Mamma with a painful look. "But I didn't think the slip of paper was for any money! The *baas* just said it was a surprise. Don't speak as if you're so high and mighty! We have to do what the *baas* says!" He reached for his coffee, sloshed half of it in the saucer and took intermittent sips while blowing. "But what am I telling you all these things for?"

"Because I want to know, my man," she said, totally unmoved by his outburst.

"You're too suspicious, Wiesie," he continued in a quieter tone. "Sure enough the white man kicked us off his farm because of our child's education. But who doesn't, huh? Show me a white man who allows teachers and doctors to live on his farm!" Pa got back in his chair and struggled to relight his pipe.

Mamma almost laughed in his face. "Don't be ridiculous, Attie. Who will stay on a farm if he can become even a teacher or a bricklayer? No one! The Boers are afraid that if our children get education then there won't be anybody left to work their farms. But it isn't so. I for myself liked the life on the farm. If things can be better, like a living wage, a way out of the poverty and filth and continual drunkenness, then who would want to leave? But maybe the whole system is built in such a way that there can be no living wage."

"Now you're getting too deep for me, Wiesie," he said. "I don't understand these things that you're talking about."

"All your life, all your life you've been sweating and labouring away for a penny ha'penny. And all for what?"

"For you and the children, Wiesie." He briefly glanced in my direction. I pretended to look about the living-room. "For you and the children. I never had much education, but with these two hands I have slaved to keep this family together. And with your help I have. Are you blaming me now for what might have been? That I might've been smarter and more educated so I could fight the law and the government from here to Pretoria to live a better life and get a better deal? Where do I start to find out if even the first five shillings and sixpence that I got thirty years ago was my due payment, never mind the five hundred Rand? If you want it, then you can have it." He reached into his back pocket and withdrew a thick wad of bills. "Here! You want it? Then you can have it!" He threw the bills at her.

She ducked and the money slowly fluttered all over the kitchen. Ignoring the bills all around her, she scolded him. "It's not your money I want. What I want to tell you is this. Every person on this earth of God has the right to know whether the dealings he has made are fair and just. We are no different from anybody else in that respect. Not even from the white people."

"So you want to go on harping on this thing for the rest of your life?"

"No, at the end of my days I want to be able to reckon, and think that my deal was not so rotten."

RESETTLEMENT

OOM ADRIAAN LIMPED INTO THE SHADE OF A PATCH OF bluegum trees and sat down against the nearest trunk. A few turtledoves flitted about in the branches overhead. In the distance, he could see the white pick-up truck with GG licence plates kicking up a cloud of dust even as the vehicle left the tarred road of the mission station. He had been walking all over the station this morning and pointing out the various structures, *kraals* and cultivated fields to the government man in sunglasses. Clipboard in hand, the man had asked more questions than yesterday. Although this young man with the red handlebar moustache had spoken Afrikaans, a language common to both, Oom Adriaan had had some difficulty with questions phrased in technical jargon. The turtledoves continued their cooing in the early summer heat.

This trudging about the place had left him terribly short of breath. He wondered if the white man was trying to save government petrol or merely showing off his youthful prowess. After Oom Adriaan clambered off the back of the Ford at seven this morning, he had to run to keep up with the younger man's swift pace. A few times, when Oom Adriaan was fit to collapse, the other prodded him on with, "Come on, old man! The sun doesn't stand still." Throughout the whole morning he was only referred to as "old man." Oom Adriaan, for his part, refused to call the white man "Baas" or even "Meneer." Instead, whenever he had to speak to him he referred to him in the third person as if he were something far removed from the immediacy of their tasks.

Oom Adriaan removed his broad-brimmed hat and fanned his face. From his jacket pocket he pulled a soiled, worn handkerchief and wiped his forehead. A few thunderheads loomed on the horizon but the wind was still too strong from the west. No chance of rain, he decided, with the cicadas still so noisy in this sticky heat.

Once they grew silent, he knew, then the rains weren't too far off. With this bad leg, he should have accepted the white man's offer of a ride back to the office. Instead, he had mumbled something about fixing a fence somewhere because he couldn't bring himself to clamber onto the back of the truck like a common labourer again. He tried to get up from his sitting position. A terrible pain shot up from his right knee into his hip. He fingered the leg gingerly and shifted his weight onto his left side. Better to take it easy for a while, he thought. His pocket watch showed he still had seven minutes of his coffee break left.

For a long time Oom Adriaan, like everybody else, had known changes were coming to the place. According to current rumours, the entire estate was first going to be sold to the central government of Pretoria and afterwards handed over to the still unborn Ciskei homeland. Since his own tenure as agricultural foreman began forty years ago, he had seen so many church administrators coming and going that he had lost track of them. Some had come with all sorts of ideas to improve this jewel in the church's crown of black educational institutes. There had been a few incompetents, intent on being good priests first and administrators last, who could hardly keep the place together. The only ones who had left without any fanfare were those who had made a nurse or student pregnant. Then there had been the young volunteers from Europe who had wanted to teach him a thing or two about animal husbandry or crop rotation. Through it all he had always been secure in his belief that no matter who came or who left, he would always have his job and the place would remain in church hands. Even the cornerstone at the main entrance attested to the agreement between Queen Victoria and Chief Sandile: "The land will be used by the church for the education of black children in perpetuity."

Now Oom Adriaan was no longer so sure. This new government man wanted to know how he was spending every minute in overseeing the lands and animals. He understood the reason for questions about the productive capacity of the place, but when he had to give an account of his own time he found it totally irksome. "Why?" he had asked the man in the white safari suit.

"Old man, don't you know that these are all orders from Pretoria?"

"No, I'm sorry," came Oom Adriaan's slow reply. "But do we really have to go through all this? All these years I've been working here from eight in the morning till five in the afternoon. I never kept track of how long it took me to do anything. I just did what needed doing."

"Is that so?" came the reply from the white man. He pointed a finger at Oom Adriaan and continued in a threatening tone. "Well I'm also here just to do my job. If you have questions to ask, then you'd better go to Pretoria and ask the minister there. Okay?"

There was no response from Oom Adriaan. He simply stared over the white man's shoulder at the blue mountains in the distance. The central government was making all these plans for people who had probably never seen the homeland in their entire lives. As for him and his family, there were no plans at all. He wondered if perhaps the church would be willing to accommodate him somewhere else.

A few times he had been to visit relatives in the barren, treeless townships of Bonteheuwel, Paarl East and Schauderville. There was just no way he could see himself living a hand-to-mouth existence under such overcrowded conditions. For years his hopes had been to be pensioned off and to build himself a small, comfortable bungalow near the foothills of the Amatola Mountains. But if all that area was going to become part of a homeland for Xhosa speakers, then he would surely not be able to live there at all. Worse still, if he were sent packing now, there wouldn't even be a pension in two years time. He wondered whether he should speak to the church people. After all, they were his employers and his church leaders had always been outspoken critics of apartheid. Their opposition to the hated system was always heralded in newspapers, parliamentary discussions or meetings.

Recently a young, white churchman had joined the mission staff. It was rumoured he was widely travelled and showed himself a fierce opponent of apartheid in his sermons. Everybody knew this priest made weekly trips to the newly created resettlement camp nearby, where he distributed cash to the poor and destitute. Oom Adriaan always felt uncomfortable in his presence. Perhaps it was because the priest refused to speak Afrikaans, or maybe Oom Adriaan was also partly to blame. Maybe, he thought, I should approach him first while he's still such a new man. After all, I have been here longer than any of these churchmen.

This positive notion gave him new strength. The excruciating pain which had earlier gripped his lower right leg was now replaced by numbness. He checked his pocket watch again and saw he had been sitting right through his lunch hour as well. He stretched out his arms on both sides and tried to heave himself up through sheer force. Halfway up against the tree trunk he suddenly found he had no strength left to push himself up all the way. With a shudder he felt the pain shooting from the knee to his hip again. Pearls of sweat formed on his forehead and, with a groan, he sank back on the bed of bluegum leaves. The few twigs scattered nearby looked too brittle to support his weight. After a few seconds he saw exactly what he needed. About ten feet away, protruding from the base of a tree at an angle, was a sapling no thicker than his wrist. Using his hands, he started slithering across the crackling leaves. In the treetops the turtledoves became quiet again, but the cicadas kept up their shrill cutting of the afternoon heat. Using the weight on his good side, he tore the sapling free from the base. He picked the sapling free of leaves. He now had a staff about the same height as his five and a half foot frame. After testing the staff for a few steps, he found it made his progress much easier. He hobbled back to pick up his hat at the base of the tree.

Halfway to the breeding pen he came across the young white priest riding a Suzuki. For a minute Oom Adriaan was undecided whether to raise his problem with this man. He looked so terribly young in cowboy boots and jeans. However matters were quickly decided for Oom Adriaan as the motorcycle came to a stop. Above the putter of the machine, the priest greeted him benignly and wanted to know where he had been all morning. Danile, the assistant foreman, had mentioned something about a problem with a calving cow earlier in the day.

"Afternoon, Father!" Oom Adriaan started in a high-pitched tone while removing his hat. "I had a problem with my right leg, Father."

"And is it better now?" the priest asked. "Otherwise you'll have to take time off and see the doctor." He revved his engine impatiently because Oom Adriaan blocked the way. A sudden breeze wafted the fragrance of an expensive cologne on the afternoon air.

"Father!" Oom Adriaan started again. He folded and rolled the brim of his hat.

"Yes?" The priest raised one foot on a pedal. Above the black-rimmed glasses his eyebrows twitched. Was he in a hurry to get to the resettlement camp? There were rumours of an overseas filming crew that had arrived yesterday.

There was so much Oom Adriaan had wanted to discuss with this priest. Or, for that matter, anybody else who would just listen to him. For a long time he had compared this present government policy of dumping people in the homelands with that of the British administration a hundred years earlier. At that time his own grandfather and other Khoikhoi leaders had led an armed uprising against the government, when the Kat River settlement became overcrowded. He saw a similar rebellion occuring here in a few years' time. He was not a learned man but he prided himself on his ability to remember and to understand.

The priest switched off the engine. The impatient look remained on his face. Seeing this, Oom Adriaan dismissed his earlier thoughts. Besides, he reminded himself, he didn't even have enough English words to express such ideas to this man.

"Father," he started again. "Father, my English is not of the best but I still want to speak." His sweaty hand had become slippery on the grey bark of the stick and he quickly wiped his hand on the side of his pants before he resumed his grip. He stared at the priest as if waiting for permission to continue.

"Then what is it you want to say?" came the high-pitched voice. "What was your name again?"

"Adriaan, Father."

"You mean Adrian. Not so?"

Oom Adriaan had nothing against somebody anglicizing his name, but he felt this white man was deliberately being English and superior.

"Yes, Father." This was no time to argue petty issues. He shaded his eyes from the harsh glare of the sandy path.

"Well speak, Adrian! I don't have all day you know."

He saw the priest taking in his worn, cast-off clothing with a twitch of his nostrils, almost as if the man had smelled something disagreeable.

"No, Father. It is just this . . . " He felt himself growing hot again as the English words failed to come on demand. "Father, see," he forced the words out. "The mission is going to be give . . .

given over to the government." With one smooth movement he replaced his hat and wiped the sweat from his forehead with the back of his hand.

"I know that, Adrian. But it's not us," the priest continued, gesturing to include the entire mission station. "It's not us, the church, who are doing this willingly. We," he added, pointing to himself as if explaining things to a deaf mute five-year-old, "are forced to do this by the government in Pretoria. And we're not giving the place over to the government. We're selling it to them."

"Yes, I know so Father."

"Since you know so much, then why are you coming to me?" He gripped the handlebars again.

"Father, what I want to know is this. Is it possible that I and my family can stay on after the selling is over? I've only got two more years before my pension."

"Now Adrian, you speak like a man who knows very little. Don't you know that we all have to go? Even you too. Or do you want to become a sell-out to the government? No, Adrian, we're all in the same boat together."

A flash of total bewilderment crossed his face. "I know, Father, but still . . . I really don't know, Father. Where do I go from this place? All my life I've worked and lived here on the mission and I don't know any other place." He knew he was begging this white man, but his whole future was at stake here.

"Now you see what I always say," the priest declared. "You Coloured people are always concerned with yourselves only. Never even worried about the next man or issues of national importance. What do you think is going to happen to me? Have you ever thought about my own future after this?" The priest kicked a pedal and the Suzuki roared to life again. Oom Adriaan stumbled in the narrow, sandy path and almost fell as he tried to block the motorcycle. A blinding white pain shot through his right leg and he suppressed it with a loud grunt. However, anger had given him a confidence he had never known before.

"I have thought about these things Father!" he shouted, hobbling on one leg. "Surely as a man of the cloth the church will get you some other church to . . . " His words disappeared in the roar of the engine.

The priest released his grip on the throttle slightly and the machine uttered small puffs of white smoke. "Now don't you come to me with such statements, Adrian," the priest said, jabbing his finger in the air. "You have absolutely no right to speak like that at all!"

"But Father —!"

"No, Adrian!" The priest made a deft move around Oom Adriaan and stopped a few feet away. "Go on your knees," he shouted over his shoulder, "and pray that salvation will come and this place not become part of the grand apartheid scheme!"

Oom Adriaan started limping off in the direction of the breeding pens. He stopped in his tracks. Turning around slowly, he started swearing in Afrikaans at the back of the priest riding off in the distance. "You fucking dog of a son of a bitch! Jesus Christ! You bastard son of a whoring mother!!" The words fell in a sonorous torrent from his tongue.

Exhausted, he spat contemptuously in the dirt. His tired eyes lit up with new life even as he turned and started limping toward the mission's office buildings. He'd never thought of resigning from this bloody place before, but this was it. For once in his life he was going to decide his future for himself. To hell with this place. To hell with the faith he used to have in the kindness of the church. They had only made plans for themselves. He wasn't going to wait for them to tell him it was time to leave. He would hand in his resignation right now.

In the distance the cicadas still screeched.

SOMETIME FOR SURE

CHAWE STEPPED WITH AN AIR OF SELF-IMPORTANCE FROM THE taxi. He ignored the driver's protests and slammed the door firmly shut behind him. The driver opened his door as if to follow him but, on seeing Chawe wobble back toward the car, rolled down the window and waited.

In his whole life Chawe had never run away from an argument. He had always prided himself on his exact use of words, and no matter what the problem was, he could always talk himself out of it. Now he pushed his brand-new green felt hat to the back of his shiny, bald head and faced the driver squarely. A group of ragged children playing in the dirt nearby caught his eye. Always ready to impress an audience, he pulled a gleaming silver pocket watch from his vest pocket and spoke without removing his eyes from the timepiece. The smell of stale liquor fanned the driver's face. "Now be a good boy and come back for your money this afternoon," Chawe said. "You know that I've come from far and the banks haven't opened yet."

Behind him, the early morning sun cast long shadows and flickered on the silver chain. The children abandoned their game and crowded around the car. He pocketed the watch and stepped back to wait for some sign of agreement from the driver.

The driver took in the pinstriped suit, lingered a while on the patent leather shoes and then stared directly at the piglike, gleaming black stub of a nose. Without shifting his eyes, he switched off the motor, adjusted his seating and spread one arm along the passenger seat. Stifling a huge yawn, he said in a deadpan voice, "Just go and ask your wife, Chawe. I can't come back for a mere fifty cents."

The little man now gripped both lapels of his jacket and pushed out his huge belly. "Don't you tell me what to do, young man!"

Chawe said. "I'm twice your age! What happened to your respect, huh? What do you take me for?! I'll pay you this afternoon and not a minute earlier." His last words came out in a wheezy tone. Some of the children had started giggling knowingly but, intent on having the last word in this argument, he ignored them.

He heard the driver clearing his throat as if to say something. A gob of spit caught Chawe between the eyes. At the same time there was a roar of a car engine jumping to life, and a rain of gravel hit him. Numerous shrieks cut through the early morning air. He pulled a white handkerchief from his breast pocket while loudly cursing the taxi driver's mother's privates. Chawe looked from behind the handkerchief and realized the children's shrieks had switched to jeering laughter. This time he cursed their own mothers' privates while dusting himself furiously. There were curious stares from a few windows and he started waddling away in embarrassment. Fresh laughter came from the children.

This was not the way Chawe had planned things. Perhaps he shouldn't have taken the taxi in the first place. Right at the railway station he had seen that boy had no respect. The least the son of a whore could have done was to give him a free ride. He wondered what had happened to all his old acquaintances and drinking buddies. Any one of them would have been thrilled to give him a ride. For a fleeting moment it occurred to him that perhaps he shouldn't have spent all his hard-earned money on the train. Still, he'd had a fine time with the young girls on this journey. He wondered what he was going to tell Esther. He paused for a minute before turning the door handle and straightened his tie. Perhaps she was not even home; otherwise the commotion would have drawn her attention. The door was locked. He knocked a few times. He took in the brand-new paint on the walls and checked the house number again. Sure it was the right place, he smiled at himself. How could he possibly mistake his own council house? So this was where all his money had gone. Instead of saving for a rainy day, Esther was always spending. He was just about to give up when a pretty little thing in a starched apron opened the door.

"Yes?" she inquired tartly.

"And who are you?" Chawe wanted to know. His authoritative tone took command of the situation.

"Oh." She curtsied slightly on high-heeled shoes. "I'm the maid for Missus Esther. But the missus, she's not home right now."

"Never mind," Chawe bellowed. "I'm the husband of the house." He pushed past her.

"But the missus she said —" the girl protested. She covered her nose.

"Never mind the missus. I'm the man of the house here. Did she never tell you about me?"

"No, I'm sorry sah. The missus neva told me anything."

"Well, I'm back now. How long have you been working here?"

"Three, four years, sah." She shut the door behind her.

Chawe made himself comfortable on a brand-new couch while the maid watched him suspiciously. Things have surely changed, he thought. He had expected some changes, but the whole house seemed unrecognizable. He should have written to Esther that he was coming but he had wanted to surprise her. Now he was the surprised one. How could she possibly have afforded to buy all this furniture on the thirty Rands he sent her every month? She should be knee-deep in debt. And what was this maidservant doing here? She was standing stiffly as if waiting for new orders. If he hadn't been so worn-out, he would've tackled her right now. "And where's your home town, *yinthombi*?" he asked. This seemed to put her at ease.

Curtsying again, she answered with a slight smile, "Lusikisiki, sah." Well, this young woman had not been spoilt by the city life. At least she still showed some respect.

"Now where has the missus gone to?" he asked. He removed his jacket.

"The missus had to go with some white clients, sah."

"What?" he wheezed, straightening his legs. "What white clients is this?"

"Oh sah," she answered, staring at her feet, "the missus she went to read their tea leaves."

So this was how his wife had been making money. No wonder there was all this brand-new furniture and pictures of half-naked women on the walls. She sure was doing well. He felt himself immensely proud of his wife's achievements. Still he felt that, as master of this house, he should have been consulted. It was good for Esther to have made money, but she should have got his permission first.

"Now that you mention tea, please make me a cup. I'm parched."

"Yes, sah," the maid replied and left the room. He suddenly decided to follow her to the kitchen. The girl eyed his constricted breathing sympathetically. "I won't be a minute with the tea, sah? Or maybe you would like something stronger?"

"No thanks," he muttered, "I'm just looking around."

From a gleaming white fridge she took a cup of cream. A kettle sat on a brand-new Hotpoint stove.

He wandered off to the bedrooms. Each of the two bedrooms now contained four beautifully made-up beds. Like cubicles, the beds were divided by flimsy curtaining suspended from the ceiling. He sniffed in the air. There was a distinctive smell of male bodies and, more faintly, the odours of stale sex and perfume. He wondered if she had taken in boarders, or what was happening here? The idea that his home was used as a brothel was too far-fetched. Besides, Esther seemed to hate the very notion of sex. In any case, he was going to sort it out with her when she came home. He never could stand the idea of sharing a house with anybody except his immediate family. It suddenly occurred to him what he had missed when he had entered the front door. He rushed back to the living-room but, instead of their wedding photograph, there was a picture of a half-naked woman riding a tiger. All his high school diplomas and correspondence school certificates had been replaced by watercolours of landscapes and ferocious beasts.

The maid brought a tea tray to the living-room but he motioned her away. On second thought he called her back. "What is your name, young woman?"

"Thembeka, sah," she said, balancing the tray on her hip.

"Now, Thembeka, what is happening here in my house?"

"I don't know . . . I mean. What do you mean, sah?"

"Are there other people living here in this house beside my wife?"

She suddenly became tense. "I don't know, sah. I knock off at one o'clock, sah. Maybe the missus can tell you, sah."

Chawe realized he was not going to get anywhere with this maid and sent her away. With his head in his hands he realized his presence here had been obliterated as if he had never existed. He walked back to the bedrooms and started checking out the wardrobes. No, there were no shoes or clothes belonging to him or any other man. Only rows upon rows of fashionable women's shoes and dresses. He flung himself down on the nearest bed and shut his eyes.

Five years earlier his wife had laughed derisively when he had mentioned he was going to go to Port Elizabeth.

"What for?" she giggled. She was straining to hear the drama on the short-wave channel.

"To make money," Chawe wheezed. He was drumming his fingers on the kitchen table.

"Stop that," she said, ignoring his reply.

Dutifully he stopped his drumming. He started to speak again but her attention was with the Monday afternoon drama. He quietly picked his teeth with one thumbnail and stared above her head at the opposite wall. A Sunlight soap commercial, accompanied by hisses and crackles, signalled the end of the programme.

"You know, Esther," he ventured again.

"Can't you ever wait till the story is done?" she screeched back at him. He got up from the table and stared out the small kitchen window. Behind him he heard the radio switched off with a loud click.

"You good for nothing!" she shouted at his back. "You're always spoiling my pleasure because you have no joy of your own! Nobody comes to visit you except for your drinking cronies. And no job! No job whatsoever! Go on looking outside! There's no men to be seen out there. They're all at work!" With increasing anger she continued: "I had thought I married a man with education and a will to work. But what I've got is a shit-assed man. Half-baked in everything and no good at all."

To Chawe there was nothing new in this outburst. They had been through all this before. Still it hurt when she belittled his attempts at earning a living. In fact, he already felt he had lost the argument, with Esther calling him a shit-assed man. He concentrated on two dogs going through a mating ritual in the street. The bitch now licked the dog's penis to a walking stick hardness and frequently moved her rear end in his face. Chawe felt a faint stirring in his loins. Earlier in their marriage Esther always rushed him to get things done and over with. Now he couldn't remember when last he had had sex with her. He suddenly realized she had started shouting at him. A bulge showed in his pants as he turned to face her.

"Sis!" she shouted, staring with glassy eyes at his pants. "What have you been looking at, huh?"

She quickly moved her small, skeletal frame to within a few

feet of him and tried to look over his shoulder. Chawe didn't budge from his position one step. Esther made a grab at him but stopped midway. He saw she couldn't bring herself to pull him out of the way. Not with this thing pointing at her. She went back to the table.

"So what's with this going to Port Elizabeth?" she asked quietly while retying her *doek*.

He felt his erection grow weak and the fire leaving him. "They say . . . they say that General Motors has opened a new car plant there and people from New Brighton are getting rich." His reply was hoarse.

"And you plan on going there and getting rich yourself?" She giggled a little at the thought. "Isn't that the place which you left years ago to come and make your money here? Be your age, Chawe. At forty-five you want to go like a young man and look for your fortune?"

"But things have changed, Esther. That place is no longer backward . . . " he quietly countered and returned to the table.

"There's lots of work here, but you're just lazy." She got up from the table and scooped a cup of water from the water pail. Through the window she saw the street deserted except for two dogs engaged in a tug of war. Chawe eyed her suspiciously, but she continued between quaffs. "Now what are you going to tell the white people at General Motors? Surely they're going to ask you if you understand cars and you know yourself that you've never driven a car in your whole life." She went for a fresh cup of water. "Speak up, Chawe! Speak up like a man!"

"Well," he ventured hesitantly. "Maybe I could be a foreman or a quality control clerk."

"But you've never done these jobs before. Have you?"

"Surely they can teach me how to do it!" He felt as if this woman was making things deliberately difficult for him. Did she want him around the place to play boss over him forever?

"At your age the *abalungu* will have no time for you," she hissed viciously.

"But do you want us to go on living on your meagre earnings from piano lessons?"

"Don't you ridicule my work. I could still have been a school teacher, but through you and your politics I had to give it up. 'No,' you said, 'it's Bantu education and it's useless to be a tool of that apartheid system.' Now look at all these Bantu education teachers.

They're nobody's tools. They drive big cars and have big houses and I am the fool. I wish I had never listened to you and your white liberal friends."

This was the most painful part: to be reminded of his erstwhile liberal friends. With these people he had firmly believed that, through the qualified franchise, he and other aspiring blacks would one day have their rightful place in South African society. Somehow it seemed impossible to them that the state could promulgate the Political Non-Interference Act, which prohibits political gatherings across the colour bar. Chawe was flabbergasted when men like Alan Paton and Edgar Brookes cried over this new act but did nothing to counter it. When the white liberals disappeared into their shiny corporate offices, they effectively abandoned him to the merciless taunting of his fellow blacks.

Somehow he had convinced her there was money to be made at the car factory. Or had he? Maybe she'd been the one who had relented and had given him a chance to be a wage earning man again. On his first day in Port Elizabeth he had landed a job. Of course it wasn't what he had wished for, but he was told there was room for advancement. And so he had assembled car headlights for five years. Each month he sent thirty Rands home and kept the remaining twenty-five for his own livelihood. Finally he just got sick of the low pay and long hours and decided to quit. Surely his parents had not scrounged and saved for his education only to see him assemble car headlights? Lying spread-eagled on the bed, he mused that his life thus far had been a series of episodes. He wondered if other people also led such lives. Most men he knew had been working at the selfsame job for donkey's years. Their lives were strung out between workplace and home and they never even went for holidays anywhere. When they did get vacation, they normally made a nuisance of themselves around the house until their wives and children wished they never had a break from work. Why was he so different?

The maid appeared in the doorway with a bottle of Lion lager on a tray. She was wearing fresh make-up. He sent her away as he was in no mood for booze or sex now and shouted at her to shut the door behind her. He needed to think.

Somehow his parents believed that a highschool education in itself would be a lever. It would propel their only child from the mission school into the white man's world of consumer goods, money and the attendant respect from fellow blacks. Well, he thought, education was no magic formula for getting things in life. You have to keep on working to secure your upward mobility. But then education also brought its own problems of questioning values, concepts and beliefs. His own education had propelled him into issues which his parents had never even dreamed of. With his high school certificate he could even qualify to vote in the white man's elections, while others could vote merely because they had fifty pounds sterling in the bank or a residential plot in the city. He addressed issues in the white man's own language. Of course the law forbade him from standing as a candidate, but he was a much sought after canvasser at election time. He remembered the headiness of victory celebrations and the multiracial parties that followed. Among liberal whites he was considered a rising star who could debate issues, policies and beliefs with the best of them.

In retrospect, he felt that the missionaries had taught him to question too many things. The holy fathers had held up for scrutiny his own childhood belief in witchcraft, the laws of the land and everything in between. And somehow there was no room left for God. Of course he had been given a fair dose of the Book of Common Prayer and a catechism which should have prepared him for a life of a permanent believer. But wasn't it paradoxical, he thought, that the self-same monks who taught him the theory of evolution and Newton's laws also whispered in hushed tones about the mysteries of the Transfiguration at Easter? Contrary to the holy fathers' wishes, he found more common ground between the ideas of Plato and Marx in the creation of an ideal society. But this did not last very long.

Disbelief required no act of faith, no rigours of mental anguish. While belief might have honed his mind and acts of contrition his body, disbelief and its accompanying cynicism spread his hips, thighs and stomach. Soon he no longer even went to church. Instead of becoming a teacher as his parents had wished, he planned on becoming a tailor. The job of apprentice tailor lasted no longer than a month. He was one of the first in the township to start wearing the ready-made polyester suits from Hong Kong.

"I can see bad days ahead for you," he told his employer, Max. He was a wizened old man in steel-rimmed spectacles. "Soon everybody will be wearing these ready-made suits and what will become of tailoring? I see no future in the business. This suit you see," Chawe said while removing his jacket, "is wrinkle free." He slowly wrung it like a piece of laundry to the startled looks of the other apprentices. "I will even knot the sleeves and afterwards it will regain its original shape." After tying and untying the sleeves, he laid the jacket on the counter. Like a magician he continued, "And now I will put it back on and not a wrinkle will show. This is the cloth of the future." With a flourish he put the jacket back on and flattened the lapels for added effect. "If you want to, I can show you that the same thing can be done with the pants."

Max was the only one who studiously ignored his demonstration and continued with his sewing. It was Mfundo, Chawe's boyhood friend, who had spoken: "So what do you want us to do?"

The youthful Chawe thrust out his shoulders and placed both hands in his pockets before answering. "I am not telling you what to do. As for myself, I see no future in tailoring."

Suddenly Max had had enough. Only the width of the counter stopped the man from attacking him physically. "Well then," Max said, "get the hell out of here, you and your imitation polyester." He pulled out the cash drawer and counted out Chawe's weekly wage. "Here's your wages. Just fuck off, you lazy bum."

Like a prophet of old, Chawe insisted on having the last word. He swiped the money from the counter and shouted from the doorway, "I will go. But do not say that I didn't warn you about the perils of the capitalist marketplace!" Behind him he heard Max dismiss his words as jawbreakers coming out of a head of shit but Chawe felt there was nothing more for him to say.

Was it really Chawe's fear of the new industry that time, or had he just grown bored with tailoring? He wished he had known. To everybody's surprise, Chawe did not start selling polyester suits. Instead, he opened a funeral parlour with assistance from a rich uncle. His public excuse for this failure was that the community couldn't afford his fancy coffins. Personally, he couldn't stand the thought of washing and cleaning the dead.

And so it had gone from tailor to undertaker, to teacher (for one day) to political canvasser and finally assembler of headlights. Was there no job that would occupy him like a calling?

The sound of the door handle turning brought him back from his musings. He wondered if it were the maid again. He wouldn't mind having that beer now. A woman, resplendent in an elaborate kaftan and west African headgear, stepped into the room. It took him a few seconds to realize it was Esther. Struggling to get up from his prostrate position, he beamed from ear to ear. "Hello, my dearest," he said, stretching out both arms.

"What do you want here?" she hissed back at him. "Get out of here. Go away. I don't want you here. You're a disgrace and a failure. And get off that bed, you pig!" Behind her a few young women, less resplendent but more beautiful, appeared in the doorway.

"No, Esther, please," he begged, half crouching in the middle of the bed. "Please let me explain."

"You have nothing to explain, you useless dog!" she shrieked. "Just go and die so I can bury you."

"But I still want to tell you about your mother and sister in the Ciskei," he pleaded, sliding to the floor.

"Never mind my relatives. I will talk to them when I want to." From one of her embroidered sleeves she pulled three ten Rand notes. "Here, buy yourself a ticket and go back where you came from."

He had no strength to refuse this generous offer. Where were the arguments he had been thinking about earlier? He should be fighting her for running a brothel in his house and now he found himself stretching out both hands to receive the money.

"Thank you, Esther. Thank you." A small spark flickered at the back of his mind when he saw the pitying look of Thembeka, the servant girl. "But . . . but really, is this the way that you are . . . s . . . sending me . . . a . . . away?" He stuttered appealingly at the whole group in the doorway and held out the banknotes as a sign of his wife's callousness. The girls refused to become involved in this domestic dispute and their eyes looked everywhere else than at him. Only Esther's eyes bore like blazing coals into his own.

Her swift movements were lost to him as she gripped a long-necked vase from a pedestal. "Get out, you dog!" she screamed, smashing the vase over his head. A kaleidoscope of forgotten baptisms and funerals flashed through his mind while the cold water and flower perfume assaulted his senses. Picking up a ten Rand note from the floor, he wiped the water and blood from his eyes. The giggling girls parted when he stumbled through the doorway. "Remember the sins that are visited on the houses of harlots!" he screamed and ran from the house.

SHARING A TRIP TO THE SEA

IT WAS LATE FRIDAY AFTERNOON WHEN JUFFROU KALAMADIEN finally got a chance to bring her attendance register up-to-date. Department rules stipulated that entries had to be made daily, but the switch to this new Coloured Affairs curriculum had upset things so much that she despaired of the slow learners. She adjusted her glasses and settled her thin, spinsterly frame comfortably in the chair.

"Petrus Januarie!" she suddenly shouted. "Were you at school on Tuesday?" There were four Petruses and six Johns in her class so she'd grown into the habit of using both names to avoid confusion.

"*Ja*, Juffrou?" came a plaintive little voice from somewhere in the middle rows.

"And stand up when I'm talking to you! Were you at school on Tuesday?" she repeated. There were several thumps as the eight-year-old bumped his knees against the desk and his slate crashed to pieces on the floor. The boy whimpered while repeating his earlier answer.

"You're sure?" she said leaning her elbows on the table.

"*Ja* . . . Juf . . . frou," he stammered through tears. She suddenly remembered it was on Tuesday they had switched to the new readers and she continued mercilessly. "Then can you tell me what lesson we read that day?"

The boy wiped his eyes on his sleeves and stared at her blankly. Suddenly a cacaphony of voices sprang up around him. "He's lying, Miss! He wasn't here, Miss! He's lying, Miss!"

"Quiet!" she roared. Instantly the class resumed copying from the blackboard while the lone Petrus waited for permission to pick up the shards of slate. She decided to give him the benefit of the doubt. No point, really, in crucifying him now. In this present state he probably couldn't remember what he'd been doing that morning. What with the broken slate, he was sure to get a spanking at home. "Sit down, Petrus."

On all fours the boy started picking up the pieces and tried mounting them inside the wooden frame. She knew it was useless but she let him be.

Her eyes swept over the rest of the class. Although she had ignored John Malgas's habit of pinching the little girls' bottoms on previous occasions, what she now saw at the back of the class was totally obscene. Her prize pupil, Patricia, was staring fixedly at the boy.

"John Malgas!" she thundered.

There was no reply. The glassy-eyed twelve-year-old continued to expose himself in pencil hardness to the red-faced girl in the the next bench.

"John Malgas!" she repeated louder. "Get yourself over here right now!"

"Yes, Miss," came the agonized reply. He struggled to rearrange his clothing and started hobbling, as if on three legs, toward her desk.

"I don't know what you're showing to Patricia there, but you'd better come here so I can have a look too." She gripped the three-foot long cane on the desk and saw that the chubby little nine-year-old girl was quite confused. Red-cheeked with embarrassment, Patricia had dropped her head on the desk and sat with her knees clamped tightly together.

Totally absorbed in their work, the rest of the class seemed oblivious to what was happening until she started lashing John. Immediately speculation rose from two noisy mouths as to what was happening. "Johannes Atlas!" she shouted in midstroke. The two mouths snapped shut in midair. "And August September! If I hear so much as a squeal from either of you again . . . !" And she finished thrashing the boy's buttocks for a total of ten times.

"Now write ten times on your slate," she said to the wincing boy, rubbing his behind, " 'I shall not be rude in class.' " A bit short of breath, she got back into her chair. She didn't particularly like caning the children; besides it wasn't good for her heart to overexert herself. But with fifty children there was no way she was going to maintain discipline without corporal punishment.

She marked off the rest of the attendance register and then

pulled a circular from her desk drawer. After she read it, she cleared her throat to speak. Except for the most ignorant, just about everybody knew that when she did this something nice was going to be said. Ready to hear some good news, most of those in the front rows immediately put down their slate pencils and folded their arms. The inactivity swept like a wave to the farthest corners.

"Class," Miss Kalamadien started in a pleasant tone. She cleared her throat a second time. "And John Malgas, you can also put down your slate pencil for a while. Now class," she continued a pitch higher, "the school is planning a trip for us to the seaside at Somerset West." She kept quiet for a while to let this information sink into the little brains. In the same pleasant voice she continued. "The cost for this trip will be one Rand and twenty-five cents." To make sure everybody had understood her, she asked, "How much money should you bring for this trip to the sea?"

"One Rand and twenty-five cents, Miss!" came a chorus from the little throats. This time nobody got up when speaking.

She dropped to an even friendlier tone now that she had their total attention. "And for the next five weeks, each one of you must bring twenty-five cents every Monday morning." After resting for a minute, and before they could break into screams and shrieks at this news, she asked them, "How much money should you bring every Monday morning? Now say after me, 'Twenty-five cents.' "

"Twenty-five cents, Miss!" came the unified response. Even John Malgas had forgotten his earlier caning and contributed heartily to the chorus.

"And when should you bring it? Say after me, 'Every Monday morning.' "

"Every Monday morning, Miss!"

Comfortable that each and every child had understood what was said, she started working on her day plan for Monday. There was immediate pandemonium but she ignored it. Let them rejoice in the news, she thought. When the noise got too loud she had an idea. Looking around at the walls, she soon found what she needed. Between a profusion of maps, pictures of exotic peoples in distant lands and charts of rules of grammar, there was a picture of two blond children building the most perfect sand castle topped with numerous little flags. In the background a white ship sailed on the bluest sea imaginable while a few seagulls hovered nearby. Strange that none of the children were looking at it, she thought.

Then she caught little Petrus Januarie staring at the same picture. When he met her gaze, he looked at his slate guiltily as if he had done something wrong. Getting up from her desk, she called on John Malgas to carry the chair over to the wall. The rest of the class was still as noisy as ever except for little Petrus, who was anxiously waiting to see what would happen next. Over her shoulder she gave him a sly little grin while she removed the thumbtacks. Confused, he didn't return her smile but instead made a renewed attempt to fit the jagged pieces into the wooden slate frame.

Back at the blackboard, she rapped the desk for attention. "Now class, I want you all to look at this picture very carefully. What do you see?"

Numerous voices shot up. "The sea!" shouted a few. "A ship!" called another. "Children playing!" others retorted. She let them exhaust themselves until even the most observant ones had nothing more to say.

"Now, I want you to wipe your slates clean and write down the things that you would need for a trip to the sea. Did you get that?" There was no response. She turned to the blackboard and wrote down the numbers one to ten in vertical sequence. Next to number one she wrote "swimming trunks." "Now I want each of you to write the other things that you will need for a trip to the sea. Look at the picture, and you will see some of them. If you have problems with a word, raise your right hand and I will write it down for you. Okay?"

"*Ja*, Juffrou!" came a multitude of replies. She knew Patricia was probably halfway through her assignment already. The child had regained her composure and was printing on her slate with the intensity of one who enjoyed what she was doing. On her left, John Malgas was equally busy, biting his tongue with effort.

"Patricia!" she called in an affected English voice to the only English speaker in class.

"Yes, Miss?" came the high-pitched reply.

"Please bring your slate to me."

The child bounced to the front of the class and Miss Kalamadien viewed the beautiful printing with satisfaction. "Very nicely done, Patricia. Now wipe your slate clean and lend it to Petrus. Okay?" She hugged the warm little body for a minute.

"Yes, Miss."

A hand suddenly shot up at the back.

"Yes, John?"

"How do I spell 'bottled water,' Miss?"

"Now what would you need bottled water for?"

There were several loud guffaws and giggles but he wasn't easily silenced.

"Whenever, Miss, whenever Abdullah and I go to the seaside to sell fruit, Miss, we always have to take bottled water with us. Because there are no taps and the sea water is salt, Miss," he finished proudly.

"Well, don't worry yourself about 'bottled water.' Where we're going there will be taps for drinking water." She smiled, amused. She was always impressed by the extensive vocabularies of children like John Malgas who sold fish, fruit and vegetables for the Muslim traders in their spare time. While imploring prospective customers on Saturday mornings from behind their market stalls with sing-song chants of "This is the right time to buy *snoek*, Merrim—any other time you won't enjoy this fish as much as you would today," and, "How about a few tomatoes for tonight's tomato-stew, Missus?" —at such times those children were using the Afrikaans language in its most fluid, musical form. Of course they never quite spoke like that in her presence, but their experiences did enrich their speech in class.

Every Monday morning the children, with few exceptions, brought their twenty-five cents diligently. Juffrou Kalamadien entered the amounts in a notebook. Some, the children of bricklayers and carpenters, had brought the whole amount of one Rand twenty-five on the very first day. These ones she had sent back with the reprimand that they were supposed to bring only twenty-five cents every week. There was no way she was going to allow some to behave as if they were better than the children of common labourers. Only Patricia was allowed to pay the full amount on the first day.

She noticed that for a few days there were welts from a terrible beating behind Petrus's legs. She told him to dump the one jagged piece of slate which he had kept into the garbage can, and she bought him a brand-new one from the nearby corner store.

As the day approached, there was a growing excitement among the children. Whenever she rang the bell for them to return to class after lunch, they continued to hang about in groups, holding onto somebody's story about the sea. One lunchtime she eavesdropped on a group through a back window. Sitting along the wall like sparrows in a row, several children were regaled by John Malgas about his trips with Abdullah to the sea. Chains, as his friends called him on the playground (because his father had once been jailed for beating somebody with a bicycle chain), stood like an orator facing the other boys.

"And is the sea really blue?" came a question right under the window.

"Oh yes!" Chains answered. "Every drop of it is blue, but when you take some water from it, then it looks just like tap water. Abdullah says it loses colour because the sea doesn't want any part of itself removed."

"So the sea is really alive, hey Chains?" the same boy wanted to know.

"You'd better believe it! If you're not careful," and he beat two fingers in the palm of his other hand for emphasis, "I swear to Allah the sea will pull you right inside and drown you."

A collective sigh went up from the group but the one little voice peeped rebelliously again. "I'll just tie myself to a tree with a lo-ong string and then the sea won't be able to pull me in!"

"You'd better watch out for the *blerry* sharks and stuff. They'll chew down that string and then the sea'll get you! Maybe they'll even chew off your *blerry* little cock and balls, too!" There was raucous laughter from the other children. Before she could stop the language from getting any worse, Chains suddenly started again in an almost reverential tone. "Abdullah says—"

One of the other boys cut him short. "You're always saying Abdullah this and Abdullah that. What's with this Abdullah, huh?"

"You shut your mouth you little Iblies of a pig! Abdullah is a better man than any man you know!" To the rest of the group he continued somewhat hesitantly. "Well . . . he says . . . I mean . . . Abdullah, he says that all the fishes and things are the sea's children and they do whatever it wants them to do." There were no further responses from the group while they started heading back to the school entrance.

Miss Kalamadien wondered how this Muslim, Abdullah, could have such a profound effect on a Christian child. Her own father was raised a Muslim but he became a Christian during his years as transport rider into the interior in the twenties. He had always held that the Christian religion was stronger than Islam. For herself she'd never really thought about the issue deeply because she was no churchgoer. She thought perhaps one day she would ask Chains to get this mysterious good man to come to school. Maybe she would then also have a chance to tell him about Chains's swearing and obscene behaviour.

A week before they were to go the sea, she became concerned about Petrus. The child had not contributed a penny yet. Instead of playing the Good Samaritan again, she decided she was not going to help him. It was enough she'd bought him a brand-new slate with her own money. Besides, that was an essential item. No matter how much he looked forward to this trip it was still a luxury. If he couldn't afford it, then he'd better very well stay home.

In the early morning of the big day some of the older boys animatedly described their previous visits to the sea. A few others were arguing about the shortest possible route from Paarl to Somerset West. The loudest ones were those most poorly dressed. Somehow, they wanted to deflect attention from their cast-off clothing and have the others focus on their words instead. Like other desperately poor children she had known before, they could only impress others through their knowledge. She had repeatedly told them to form five straight lines in preparation for the truck's arrival but today the children seemed uncontrollable. The younger ones' clothes were already smeared with dirt and grime from playing in the dust. She tried to get a few girls to sing under her direction. Finally near eight o'clock she took them all into the classroom because some passing drivers had shouted lewd remarks at her.

Petrus Januarie sat in his usual place with well-combed hair and with teeth brushed to a Colgate whiteness. Unlike the other children, who for the most part wore their Sunday clothes, he was dressed in his regular school outfit. The checkered shirt seemed freshly ironed and the khaki pants had creases in the legs. Otherwise he was barefoot as usual.

"Petrus!" she called. "Did you bring your money for the trip? And where's your sandwiches?" She looked around at the numerous biscuit tins and shopping bags on the other desks.

The boy quietly avoided her stare.

"I'm talking to you, Petrus!"

He got up slowly.

"Now answer me! Where's your one Rand twenty-five?"

"Juffrou . . . " The word hung in the air.

"Yes . . . ?"

"Juffrou . . . I thought that maybe . . . that maybe if somebody didn't turn up then you will let me take his place."

She laughed openly at the idea. "Now where did you ever hear such a thing? Answer me." A few stragglers suddenly came in and, amazed that the others hadn't left without them, broke into open smiles. Her stare quickly sent them scurrying for their seats. There was a clattering sound of a truck changing gears followed by a steady drone of the engine. She looked outside and saw a canopied truck with a grizzled old man at the wheel.

"Morning, Oom Dan!" she called. "All ready for the trip?"

"As ready as I'll ever be, Juffrou." He shouted back toothlessly and got out to set up a ramp. She saw him taking in her newly-ironed sundress with something like a glint in his eye.

She turned and found a whole bunch already behind her. "Get back to your desks! Right now!" There was a scurry of feet. "Now girls first. Patricia! Come over here and take the lead. See to it that everyone sits properly in the truck." She made a grab for the cane when a boy tried to trip one of the girls. They marched out so demurely, she wished she'd brought a camera for today. "Next you boys, line up here! John Malgas! You be the first. And let me know if anyone misbehaves. They'll be sent home this instant." She suddenly remembered Petrus Januarie, who sat quietly at his desk and watched the line of boys troop outside. "Okay, Petrus! You go home now. I'm sorry, but you haven't paid your bit. Here's five cents. Go buy yourself some sweets and be a good boy, hey!"

"No thanks, Juffrou," he blurted out. His bare feet slapping the floorboards, he ran out of the classroom.

"Well suit yourself then," she called after him. She shut all the windows and checked to see if anybody had left anything behind. Sure enough there was a biscuit tin which somebody in his haste had left inside his desk. After locking the door and checking it two times, she went to the back of the truck.

Down the ramp came John Malgas.

"And where do you think you're going now, boy?" she

demanded. "Get back in there right now!"

He continued climbing down with a cake tin in hand.

Her voice raised a pitch. "I said get back in there, John!"

At the bottom of the ramp the boy turned toward her. "No, Juffrou," he said. "I've let Petrus take my seat on the truck. I thought I'd let him go in my place because he's never seen the sea before. Besides, I'll be going with Abdullah to Cape Town next week."

"Well I'll be darned," she said to the quiet Oom Dan. He was waiting, ready to hoist the ramp. "That's awfully nice of him. Don't you think so, Oom Dan?"

The old man nodded mutely.

"Shut the back door, Oom Dan," she said. "Come, Chains, you can ride in front with us."

THE SECOND VISITATION

DUTIFULLY THE CHUBBY, TWELVE-YEAR-OLD BOY, PETER Willemse, read the Afrikaans newspaper report to his mother. In his high-pitched, sing-song voice he sounded out the legal terminology, rested at the commas and stopped unnecessarily long at the full stops. At his age his voice carried none of the gravity a sentencing report demanded. His tone was as neutral as if he were reading from a school textbook. The boy was suffering from a bad cold. A few times, when he thought his mother wasn't looking, he quickly wiped his nose on the sleeve of his navy-blue school blazer. Midway through the passage his tone became so nasal that his mother sent him to the bathroom.

"Go blow your nose on some toilet paper, Peter," she said. The boy scurried away and after a few loud blows returned to the newspaper.

Seated on the other side of the open-grain kitchen table, his mother resumed listening, her chin cupped in the palm of her hand. At thirty years of age she was already scrawny from numerous pregnancies and beatings. Her youth showed only in her alert and determined look.

Although the legal terms confused her, Hettie didn't stop her son to look up the meaning of the heavy-sounding Afrikaans in his school dictionary. Burdening him with requests for explanations would only slow their progress. All these terms were the white man's language, far removed from the immediacy of her life. What did matter was that she was getting a sense of what had happened at the trial. The flowery language made her realize what difficulties her two brothers had faced in court. If she couldn't understand some of it, how could they? She'd had two years of schooling and neither of them had had any.

Pouring through the curtained window, the afternoon sun cut a swath through the gloom of the kitchen. She wondered how there could still be dust floating about when she kept the cleanest council house on the whole street. She would have to start supper soon, but for now her concerns were with her brothers. She hadn't seen them in years.

Across from her Peter had grown quiet.

"Peter."

"Yes, Ma." He looked up quickly from the pictures of the two unshaven men staring at him.

"Please read the piece for me again." With a deep sigh she continued more to herself, "I wonder what came into George and Nico. They used to be such hard-working and decent boys."

"But, Ma," Peter complained, "I've already read the paper and I haven't eaten anything since I came from school. And I've still got homework to do."

She got up from the table and took a loaf of home-baked bread from the bread bin. "Now go and change into your house clothes."

"Okay, Ma," Peter answered.

"And make sure that you put your blazer properly on a hanger," she called as he disappeared into the children's bedroom. After spreading two thick slices of bread with chicken lard and apricot jam, she set the sandwich on the table and waited for him to return.

Between mouthfuls he started again with the heading, "Robber and Rapist Sentenced.

"In the Supreme Court of Cape Town (B Court) two Coloured criminals, George, 25, and Nicholaas Arendse, 18 (related), were today found guilty of having robbed seven gas stations in the Peninsula during the night of Friday, April 17 of 1962.

"The court found that George, as leader of the gang, had influenced his younger brother, Nicholaas, to commit the heinous crimes. George was sentenced to twenty years' imprisonment with no option of parole. The court found that since the offences were committed under the influence of marijuana, commonly known as *dagga*, and the normal judgement of the accused was impaired, extenuating circumstances, as submitted by the defence, would be accepted. If, however, the Crown had made a stronger argument in refuting such evidence, the court would have called for the maximum penalty.

"For his role in the robberies, the co-accused and brother Nicholaas was sentenced to six years' imprisonment of which five years were suspended. In addition, Nico, [*sic*] was sentenced to death by hanging on being found guilty on a charge of kidnapping and raping a respectable, young white woman (under section 4, subsection (b) (i) of the Immorality Act of 1952, we are prohibited from publishing the name or identity of the white victim) during the course of their robberies. Both sentences are to be served concurrently."

Peter stopped reading and looked at his mother. "Ma, does that mean he's going to be hanged and jailed at the same time?"

Hettie got up from the table and shouted out the window at her daughter: "Jackie, pick up Willy's bottle from the dirt! How many times do I have to tell you the same thing?"

Behind her the boy resumed his reading. "Advocate Ebrahim Harmse, Q.C., instructed by the law firm of Imram Mohammed, appeared for both accused. Advocate Daniel van Niekerk represented the State. Justice K.G. van Vosloosrus, assisted by two assessors, presided."

"That's enough. Just hand me the paper." She stared at the picture of her two condemned brothers for a long while. Then she took a pair of scissors from a kitchen drawer and neatly cut the article from the front page. It joined a small wad of clippings behind the framed wedding picture on the living-room wall. She shoved the rest of the paper into the burning wood stove.

They had been following the trial in the Afrikaans daily for the past week. On the first day of the trial, the court report covered almost an entire page. At other times there were just a few lines. Today, two mugshots had headed the article. She didn't really feel ashamed for her brothers' misdeeds; only, when she first got wind of it, a little pride that they had done something against the system. But now, with the finality of a court sentence in black and white, she found herself weak. A wave of memories took hold of her. Two little boys she had to care for while both her parents were at work. Nico the slow one who always ran to her when he was upset. Shielding their bodies with her own from the blows of her father. The time George had made a girl pregnant and Hettie was the first to know. The night the two of them had won the prize as best male vocalists in the whole Peninsula.

Her voice choked with emotion, she said, "Please mind the potatoes for a minute."

"Yes, Ma," Peter said, looking up from his homework.

She ran into the bedroom and slammed the door behind her. In the privacy of the room she allowed herself the luxury of weeping. This was also where she wept after assaults from her husband. She believed her children should never see their mother in weakness. Weakness was like a sickness. Uncontrolled, it spread and affected those closest to you, making them vulnerable to cruelty from others. When she felt she had wept enough, she got up and wiped her face on her apron. Running a comb through her wavy hair, she bit on her lower lip to control the small sobs still shaking her. She took one more look in the mirror and made a move toward the door but, on second thought, turned back and pulled out a bureau drawer. From under a pile of her underwear she brought up a worn baby shoe. Hidden inside was a large amount of change and a few Rands, money squirrelled away over the months for an emergency. She counted quickly. Eleven Rands and forty-five cents. More than enough for a return journey for two to Cape Town. She put the money away again.

In the kitchen again, she found Peter stirring in the pot. "No Peter, just leave it to me. You don't cook potatoes that way."

There was a sympathetic tone in his voice when he asked, "How do you cook them then, Ma?"

"Never mind," she said. "This is woman's work. Anyway, thanks for watching them."

He started busying himself with the school books again.

"Peter," she said.

"Yes, Ma?"

"How's your schoolwork coming on?"

"Okay, Ma."

"You're not writing tests or anything tomorrow?"

"No, Ma. Just some homework in social studies and math that I have to finish." He looked up from his scribbler with a quizzical expression.

She pointedly ignored his stare while she added a can of corned beef to the potatoes. Then she stirred the pot for a minute while he resumed his writing.

Suddenly she spoke again: "Peter, we're going to Cape Town tomorrow. Just the two of us. So keep this as our secret. Don't tell anybody about it. You hear?"

"But what are we going to do there?"

"We're going to visit Grandma."

"Yes, Ma," he said.

Once before, when he was six years old, Peter had been to Cape Town. Of that visit he couldn't remember much; of the journey there, even less. Huddled in a corner of the crowded third-class carriage for the most part, he had been aware only of the clickety-clack sound of the train wheels. While the train had emptied and then sped through the railyards of Ysterplaat and Paarden Eiland, he had been able to get closer to a window. Somewhere on a deserted railway platform there had been a railway worker reading a newspaper while two little white girls in bright coloured dresses had darted like butterflies between the rusted, stationary carriages. A sudden flash of shimmering blue between tall brown warehouses had been his first impression of the sea.

At his grandma's place there had been many people who were coming and going. He couldn't really recall which one was his Uncle George and which one Uncle Nico. He had stared at the newspaper photographs so long, but he couldn't bring them alive. The pictures were just of beaten, unshaven men. He could not remember which of the two men in greasy mechanics' overalls had given him a shilling that Sunday morning. Over the Sunday chicken they had spoken politics and world affairs as if they personally knew men called Verwoerd, MacMillan and Eisenhower. After lunch they had resumed their tinkering on a disembowelled truck in the backyard.

His grandmother must have changed by now. But then she had always appeared old. While the brothers had been talking, she had come into the diningroom with two bowls, custard and jelly. "Easy there now you two," she had said. "This is no time for politicking." She had worn a starched white apron over her Sunday dress and her wavy, black hair had been tied with a small bow at the back. She had given Peter an encouraging smile and a single gold tooth had flashed against her dark skin. Unlike his mother she had been quite fat (maybe his mother would grow fat too) and he had almost smothered in her hug of powder and perfume.

Earlier this week his mother had asked him if he could remember his Aunt Hilda, but there was no way he could put a face to her name. There was a beautiful woman, yes, dressed up like a movie queen he'd seen on a poster somewhere. Sometime in the afternoon a carload of people had driven up and the woman had taken hasty leave from a bunch of screaming, crying children.

Whom did all those children belong to? All of them couldn't have been the woman's. There were pretty little girls in bright dresses who made fun of his heavy, plodding Afrikaans and his lack of English. Soon a cacaphony of painful rhymes was ringing through the yard until, tormented beyond endurance, he fled into the house in search of his mother.

"Go play outside, Peter," she said. "Stop being such a baby."

This time he would surprise them all. He wasn't going to speak to them in English right away. No, he would wait until his grandma asked him about his progress at school and then he would recite some English poetry first. If she said, "What a smart boy you are," then he would ask the dumbfounded little girls with their snot noses if they had learned any poetry at school. He would ask them so many questions, they wouldn't know what to say next. Just wait and see. He would show them he could speak better English than any of them.

He and his mother would have to make sure, though, that they didn't miss the last train from Cape Town again. Last time, they missed it and had to sleep over at Grandma's place. That time his father very nearly killed his mother. This time he would make sure they got home even before his father returned from work.

Hettie was quiet when her husband came home early in the evening.

He sat down at the table and opened the English paper. "See," he said. "Crime never pays. I never liked that obnoxious manner of George, and Nico's an absolute skunk. Why can't you people ever learn to lead normal lives like all law-abiding citizens? See! Now one of them is even going to hang. If I were the judge I would've hanged both of them!" Receiving no reply from her, he opened the paper again and started reading his version of the trial in the accent of a long-forgotten English teacher.

Hettie waited until he had finished this reading. Before he could move to another section, she allowed herself to speak. Completely in control of herself, she started in a monotone. "William, I don't want us to argue. What has happened, has happened. I'm not asking you to start liking my relatives. It has been six years since I've last seen them. And all because of you—"

"Do you want to go back to your Ma?" he shouted. "Then fuck off to her."

"Please let me finish, Bill," she continued in a plaintive tone, struggling for control. "I'm only asking you to let them be. For your sake I've cut myself off from them. I'm not asking you for sympathy. Just let me do my suffering by myself. Okay?" In silence she started dishing up and sent Peter to call the other children for supper.

She turned her back to the table and wiped a tear away. Why was this man so much against her relatives? It was not that her brothers had ever wronged him. Perhaps it was just that he felt uncomfortable in their presence. Maybe it was because he wanted to be recognized as a man with an education and a trade, while her brothers were just back yard mechanics who didn't care two hoots for the niceties he observed in company. But then she loved him so dearly. He had taken her with another man's illegitimate child and given her a home. Sure, her brothers had made fun of him as "*Boerjong*" from the Boland when he'd come courting. But that was years ago.

When they got married, she had been someone special. After the wedding he had taken her all over the Paarl area to meet his relations. From dusty little hovels his uncles and aunts had come and greeted her as if she were a princess. And she, the girl from Cape Town, had done him proud. In the early years he had been impressed with the way she could set a table, be a gracious hostess, and make her children feel at ease in the company of strangers. Besides her light skin and wavy hair, she had also brought three languages—English, Afrikaans and Nama—into the marriage. But she could neither write nor read in any of them and Bill had never wanted her to speak to the children in Nama.

Somewhere during their married life something had changed. Perhaps he had grown too used to her. Perhaps she was too different to make him feel proud of her anymore. He had once rejoiced in her urbanity because it was different from the country people here. Now, like some possession, he wanted her to be like him; once he had even asked her if she were ever going to learn to speak like him. Ever since then, she'd been trying to quit talking in the free-flowing cadence of Cape Town and to adopt the plodding Afrikaans of the Boland. There was some consolation in the marriage. While a lot of other women she knew had difficulty feeding their families, she was at least assured of a weekly pay packet.

But she still missed her relatives in Cape Town.

In eleven years of marriage she had visited her mother only once. And then she and Peter went and missed the last train from Cape Town. Of course Bill accused her of having seen a man. Repeated denials only seemed to make him angrier. When she finally blurted out, "You are just *bleddy* well jealous," she got a severe beating—so badly she was hospitalized for a month. During that time he brought her flowers and hired somebody to look after the children; she found a brand-new living-room suite when she got home. Afterwards for the sake of peace she decided to cut her links with her folks.

Long after everybody had gone to bed, Hettie was still sitting in the kitchen. A few times she got up to stir the dying embers in the wood stove. There was a creak of bedsprings from one of the bedrooms.

"Jackie?" she called softly.

"Ma?"

"Better get some sleep."

"I can't sleep, Ma."

She got up from the chair, shut the stove door and blew out the candle. In total darkness she felt her way to her daughter's bed. Fully clothed, Hettie stretched herself out alongside Jackie on top of the covers. "Now try to get some sleep," she said. She drew the blankets up to the girl's chin. "You've got a long day ahead tomorrow."

"Night, Ma."

"Night, my child."

After her husband left for work, she started waking up the children. From Jackie's look she could see the girl suspected something was up. She hugged the child and felt her sleepy warm breath in the crook of her arm. A second time she shared her secret with one of her children. "And take care of the two little ones hey! After school you go over to Aunty Isabel's place and mind them till I get back."

"Are you leaving us, Ma?" There was mild alarm in Jackie's voice.

"No, my child. Besides, I'm taking Peter with me. Now get dressed and cleaned," she said. She loosened herself from the child's embrace.

"Yes, Ma. And please bring me something nice from the city. Promise?"

"Okay I promise. Now get going before I change my mind."

On the bench in the third-class carriage a youth snored loudly. His head was thrown back onto the window ledge and his exposed throat revealed a tattooed dotted line running from ear to ear. A tiny arrow pointed from the perforation to the words underneath: "To open cut here." They were very careful not to step over his outstretched legs. Under a piece of graffiti which said, "The MK was here," they found themselves a seat. Hettie made numerous attempts at conversation with Peter but finally gave up when he refused to answer in more than a monosyllable. At Cape Town Railway Station she bought two first-class tickets for the journey to the suburb. He wondered why they were now travelling first-class but refused to break the silence between them.

A quick walk from the station brought them to the end of the street where Hettie had once lived. There was very little recognizable about the house. Most of the cement plaster had fallen from the lower brickwork. The upper half, which was finished in corrugated iron sheet, showed huge rust stains through peeling green paint. In a gusty wind, a broken-down pipe screeched against the wall. An indigenous shrub, neglected for long, had grown to the height of the building and almost completely blocked the front window. Stranded in an expanse of driftsand, some vehicle, stripped to its chassis, was supported on four piles of brick. Incredibly, the driver's seat and gear lever still stuck up from the rusted wreck.

Hettie pushed at the metal tubular frame which had once served for a garden gate. Finding it impossible to open, she stooped and stepped through the opening. Peter's voice suddenly made her stop and turn. "Yes?" she asked.

"I think we're at the wrong house, Ma."

"No, Peter. This is the place."

"But Ma," he continued, unsure, "the house was different when we were here last." His mother had kept on walking and was already halfway to the front door. He followed her slowly. When he got close to her, she gripped his shoulder for a second and gave him an encouraging smile.

After her second knock they heard a thumping sound approach. A little woman opened the door and blinked into the sunlight. "Yes?" she asked, leaning on a pair of crutches. "I don't want any today."

For a moment Peter thought they they were indeed at the wrong house but then he realized this old woman was his grandmother. The once carefully combed wavy hair was now reduced to a ball of grey-flecked coir. Her face was covered in wrinkles, and where once there had been a gleaming gold tooth, only a dull pink cavity showed in her dentures.

Hettie was the first to recover. "Ma, it's me. Hettie. Hettie and Peter." She reached out to embrace her mother and the old woman let the crutches clatter to the floor.

"So you finally came, my daughter!" her mother cried. She leaned against Hettie for support. Peter picked up the crutches and followed them into the dim interior.

"Ma," Hettie said, "it's been so long that I've missed you, and now I have to come at a time like this." She led her mother to a worn couch and they sat down to console each other while Peter found a chair set against the wall. Hettie blew her nose loudly into her handkerchief. "Ma, what came over my brothers that they had to stoop so low?" She gave herself over to an outpouring of grief which Peter had never seen before. His grandmother hugged his mother, all the while saying, "It's okay. It's okay." Embarrassed by this spectacle, Peter got up and walked over to the window.

He wondered what had happened to the children. He had made all those plans to impress them and now they were nowhere to be seen. There wasn't even a toy or a stray sock or anything to show they had ever lived here. Perhaps he should ask his grandma about the children, but with all this crying going on it didn't seem right to ask. Instead he concentrated on the scene in front of him. On a branch, swaying in the wind, a chameleon was desperately trying to catch a fly trapped in cobwebs on the inside of the window. He stared, fascinated, at the spider trying to attack the chameleon's flitting tongue through the window pane. Suddenly the conversation behind him caught his attention. His mother seemed to have regained her normal self-control.

"Yes, Ma," his mother said. "Peter has been reading the paper for me everyday for the past week."

He felt himself getting warm inside with pride.

"But you shouldn't believe everything that you read in the paper, my child," his grandma said in the Nama language.

He was immediately cut off from the conversation. He had never heard this language before in his life. It was adult talk, he concluded. Maybe she was referring to something that hadn't been in the newspapers which she didn't want him to hear. He shut the adults out of his awareness and concentrated on the futile battle in front of him.

"Ma?" Hettie queried uncomprehendingly from her perch on the couch.

"You heard what I said," her mother continued in the same language. For Peter's benefit she added in Afrikaans, "Have you forgotten your first language I taught you? It is all that our family have left of our heritage. Before it's too late, better teach it to your own children."

"Yes, Ma," Hettie said in the Nama language. Her tongue was unused to the resonant profusion of clicks. "But, but to get back to the newspaper, Ma, what did you mean I should be unbelieving of the newspapers?"

"You see, Henriette, your brother George had an affair with this white woman mentioned in the papers. They were both working at a factory in Diep River. And people had warned them, not so much the woman, but George was warned by his friends about being caught for the Immorality Act. She was the one who made the plans that they should go and rob the gas stations."

"I can't believe this, Ma," Hettie reported, lapsing into Afrikaans again. "The papers said they had kidnapped her."

"All lies! All lies! My child, George had told me he planned to take the woman out of the country and marry her long before they even thought of the robberies." She spoke so vehemently that, with all the explosive clicks, her dentures threatened to fall out.

"But why is Nico then the guilty one?"

"I really don't know, my child. I really don't know. Even George swore in court that he had been the woman's lover for two years, but nobody believed him. These are the white man's courts and laws and they will always protect their own. I suppose that she was still a little in love with George and the police put her up to fingering one of them to carry the blame. Can you imagine? Our men are always supposed to rape white women."

Afterwards, on the train, Peter asked his mother when she was going to teach him the language she and Grandma spoke in. Hettie stared listlessly out of the window.

THE NEW ORDER

THE GUERRILLAS WERE HERE AGAIN LAST NIGHT. AS USUAL, THE soldiers arrived only this morning. Along the footpaths and between the shrubs, the eighteen-year-old conscripts snaked, rolled and ran from cover to cover — seemingly bent on surprising an unseen enemy.

I hang about the mission station entrance most of the time. This way everyone can see me and neither side can mistake me for the enemy. Sometimes the wind brings the sounds of gunfire and explosions but it doesn't matter to me who is winning or who is losing because I have neither friends nor enemies.

As for the guerrillas, I know most of them by name as I grew up with them. But we don't speak. To them, as to their enemy, I am merely a fixture of this abandoned institution. My insanity is taken for granted and no questions are asked or greetings exchanged. I am completely ignored.

I suppose if I had been an insane woman, the most degenerate among the soldiers would have gang-raped me. In their quest to conquer all things living, there would have been my womanness to defile. But as an insane man I have ceased to exist: a nonentity through which they stare in their search for hidden enemies. Perhaps the psychologists among them, hidden in their camouflaged uniforms, are able to detect through my body language the presence or absence of the enemy. Maybe that is why they let me live. I can see no other reason for my continued existence or for the case of bully beef the army chaplain leaves at the gate once a month.

These abandoned buildings with green moss on the roofs, walls cracked and scarred by mortars and bullets, were once a centre of activity for the entire area. From miles around, the villagers came for medical treatment and education and to find God. And I was part of life here. Now the only permanent inhabitants are a few cats, the odd snake and myself.

I remember growing up with many white people about the place. Even in my tenth year the director and his assistants were all from overseas. My mother told me they came from many parts of Europe and North America, but the ones she liked most were from Britain. These people occupied all the mission houses and singles' quarters and had exclusive use of the bathrooms and toilets. I never found it strange that my mother and all the other black teachers went home for meals while the white teachers, nurses and priests went to the mission messhall. In my childhood this mission was a huge place. There was an elementary and a high school, a Bible college and a hospital. The hospital was always the busiest place during daytime, with people coming from all over because of snakebite, broken legs, sleeping sickness, or the myriad of other misfortunes people can suffer. Our two-roomed house was at the back of the principal's house. He always called on my mother to do translation work at night.

Life was not too difficult. As a teacher's child I wore shoes, a shirt and pants. Children from the villages often came to school without shirts and always barefoot. Looking back now, I sometimes think my life was too protected. I never had to look after goats or scare the birds from the grain fields. My whole life revolved about our little corner in this foreign outpost. After school, when I had done my chores of carrying water and chopping kindling, Meme would allow me to watch the white children play. Although I was not allowed to join them, at least I could improve my English by listening to their shrill voices. Of course I can only speak now with the wisdom of hindsight. Nevertheless, for what little I gained, my loss was greater. The village children avoided me and soon I could not express myself in the lanuguage of the Oshikwanyama. But as Meme said, I was growing up for better things than the life of the villager.

In my twelfth year there were some problems. A few villagers refused to pay the cattle tax. The mission director had them flogged. Later, the police were called in because some of the black teachers refused to teach. They said they could not teach when they were refused permission to use the toilets or the mess hall. Meme said they were all Communists trying to change things. The teachers were also flogged. Although the principal told them to stay on as an example to others, they disappeared into the bush without waiting for their paycheques. In the weeks that followed, some of the grade twelve students were not seen anymore. By the end of that school term, the senior classes were so empty that the few students remaining were told to go home and wait for the following year.

On my thirteenth birthday the guerrillas came. They were not strangers at all.

There was Father Haidimbi's son, David, who used to be head altar boy. Now he was a commander, carried a grenade launcher and addressed everybody as "Comrade." Both men and women, young and old were shown the same militant respect. Only when he met his father's eyes did David falter in his commanding attitude. For the briefest of moments, the eighteen-year-old in battle fatigues was reduced by his own awareness to a mere son meeting his father after a long absence.

"*Walelepo?*" David asked. Are you well?

"*Eheh,*" his father answered. Yes.

"*Nawatu?*" Did you sleep well?

"*Eheh.*"

"*Umpiri?*" Is there peace?

"*Eheh.*"

It was almost as if David had shown traditional respect to all his people and not merely exchanged greetings with his father. The earlier scowl on Father Haidimbi's face was replaced by intense pride.

Then there was Hambalaleni. As a religious instruction teacher, she had driven the fear of God into us. Now, with her camouflaged uniform and combat boots, she seemed ten-feet tall. We children were herded into the assembly hall and told to be proud of our country, our people and ourselves. Instead of hellfire and brimstone, she told us about the revolution and how we were all going to be free. We did not even have to wait for heaven to enjoy it. It would be right here once the country was liberated. I feared for the question period which never came. Instead she asked if we had understood what she had said.

"Yes, miss!" we chorused in unison.

"I am not your miss!" she shouted back at us. "I am your

comrade!"

Some of us tried to catch the eyes of the former senior students. However, their attention was elsewhere. With their brand-new AK-47s, they stood guard all over the mission station and stopped the mission staff from going anywhere.

Afterwards they disappeared into the bushes as quietly as they had come.

Later still, everybody was called to the director's house. Red-faced with anger and embarrassment (he had been forced to kneel in a corner of his office during the entire visit), he told us in his clipped English voice to guard against evil influences. In the middle of his speech he suddenly instructed the principal to phone both the soldiers and the police. "Tell them to hurry, Dusting. They may still be able to catch these . . . eh, misfits." Then he instructed my mother to speak. She did:

"We must forget about what these wayward children said. If we do not obey the director, all these good things will come to an end. This mission will be closed and all you people will be living in the villages again. The soldiers and the police will be here soon to take statements from everybody." She turned to the parents. "Father Haidimbi, why did you not tell that boy of yours to throw away the gun and come back to school?"

To this Father Haidimbi said nothing. Some of the other parents, who also had children among the guerrillas, just shifted about and stared at their feet.

After the guerrillas' visit, some of the whites left. They were mostly the old nuns and nurses who said they did not want to become "involved." Father Thomas mentioned Malaysia, where trouble also started in such a way and his brother had had his head chopped off. Now there were soldiers at the mission everyday. With their guns, tanks and uniforms, they looked very smart and didn't appear particularly threatening. Trying to look detached from their surroundings, they seemed very bored. They always withdrew in the late afternoon to their base five miles south.

When Sister Eileen told my mother they might meet in heaven, she was broken-hearted. My mother had tended Sister Eileen in sickness, washed her clothes and cleaned her house; now she did not even think of taking us with her to England, the place she had spoken so much of. "You would have no problem in London, Khomotso," Sister Eileen had said. "There are many people from Africa. Besides, this is no place for you as you are very much English. You certainly must meet my two nieces. Jane and Jenny are always asking about you when I go home on furlough." And then she would show us some pictures of her youth and the rosy-cheeked girls. I would have liked to meet them myself and show them how well I could walk and talk like an Englishman.

Now she was gone. We were left with pictures of an English countryside and ornaments depicting lords and ladies relaxing near ponds and lakes. Perhaps that's what heaven looks like.

When David Haidimbi's band came again six months later, they were very rough. The director, principal and all the white staff were gagged and tied up in the office. As for the rest, we were herded into the assembly hall. Now he wanted volunteers to join the people's army. The whole grade twelve class stepped forward. David then called my mother to the front of the gathering. "You have been warned to leave this place comrade," he told her.

This, of course, was news to me.

"You come here with your guns and things like new toys trying to scare us," Meme answered. "Now you tell me to leave the mission. How will I feed my son when I have no work?"

"We are fighting a revolutionary war, comrade," David said. "You are either with us or against us. Why are you telling people we are just a band of thieves out to destroy the things which the white people built? Today I tell you that we are creating a new order. The mission can continue to operate but do not speak against us. We are here to liberate you from your oppression."

My mother's voice was beginning to grow shrill. "What oppression are you talking about? Here we are trying to give the children an education so they do not have to herd goats and live as their fathers lived."

David was now becoming angry. "This mission station, comrade, is only one small part of our country." He continued in his all-knowing adolescent voice. "And you are only one person in a nation of people. You have been teaching here for fifteen years. Within all that time, you have not used a toilet or the mess hall here. For all that time, you've earned a fraction of what the white

employees get paid. Why is it all of our young men do not get any
further education after this place but have to work for slave wages
on the richest diamond deposits in all of Africa? Even there they are
not allowed to use the little education they've gained in order to
work as clerks or bookkeepers. Do you not long for the day when
you can be fully in charge of this mission? That day will never
come if we do not throw off this yoke of foreign oppression.
Comrade, please believe that what we are doing is in the interest of
our country and yourself." This long speech left him quite
breathless. For a minute I thought he was just dragging on because
he did not know how to stop.

Meme tried to speak to David Haidimbi again but he simply
ignored her. "Please, David," she begged him. "Please, Comrade
David, will you allow me one more chance to stay here?"

He gave her such a sharp look that she visibly shrank into
herself. The seniors were allowed to pick up an extra change of
clothing, and they all left in the darkness.

That night, Meme was very quiet. When the principal called for
her to do translation work, she did not go.

The next day my mother disappeared. Someone had seen her
leaving the school building on the way to the library. No one saw
her arriving at the library, though. For me there was no goodbye, no
farewell. She was just gone. I tried to remember the last words we
had spoken and how she had looked at me. I can remember the
words but they had no particular significance. It was simply that I
had to remember to wash my ears thoroughly. Could this have been
a code? But then we'd never spoken in code before.

The two-room house was unbearably quiet. The pots, pans and
furniture and her clothes in the closet were so familiar and yet so
strange. Where did I start to make myself a meal? It was easy
enough to make a sandwich but cooking was an entirely different
thing. All day long I sat at the kitchen table and stared at the open
doorway. Toward supper time, one of my mother's friends brought
me a bowl of soup. She said she felt sorry for me and perhaps my
mother would come back soon. It was not my mother I missed but
the order of my day: To be able to wake up and know there was
someone to regulate my life. That was what my life was missing:
To have these utensils used and the sounds of their usage bring life
to this utter silence. At some distance I could hear the white
children playing in the compound.

The next day was Monday. I started getting my school uniform ready. Meme would have been disappointed if I had gone to school in a wrinkled shirt. While ironing, I suddenly caught myself humming her favourite hymn, "Rock of Ages."

On Tuesday the history teacher approached me. "Son, you seem to be working hard these days," he said. "Please take it easy my boy. Most of us have also lost a dear one during these times of trouble. Are you making out okay at home?"

"Yes, sir."

The schoolwork provided an escape from my mother's loss. I realized this part of the day provided me with a semblance of order I desperately needed. Into this I threw myself with fervour. I drank in all information with a thirst hitherto unknown to myself. Except when I was called by the neighbours for meals, my time was spent with school books. In the evenings, I would read until I fell asleep with Bismarck or Napoleon on my mind. I even dreamt of them. If they were alive today, then surely they would have sorted out this mess of fighting in my country with no problem at all. Marching across the country with so many thousands of footsoldiers and cavalry, they would restore peace in just a short time. They would leave in their wake beautiful buildings and bridges with a hard-working population forever thankful for this release from uncertainty. They would leave in their wake order.

Two months before my grade ten final examination the principal came to tell me he had found a job for me on the copper mines. I thought it was because of my low marks in mathematics that he wanted me to quit school and start working.

"Please, Father," I begged. "I promise to study even harder now."

"You are a good student," he said, "but we can't go on supporting you forever you know. A man must grow up and face the responsibilities of life."

"But I only want to finish my final examination."

"If you do not take the job opportunity now," he said, "it will be months before the recruiting officer from the mines comes around. Who is going to feed you in the meantime? Besides, we need your mother's house for another family."

The pictures of the English countryside and peaceful strollers receded further and further in my mind. I could not tell him I feared the unknown; instead I asked to be a teacher's aide.

"No, we can't afford to pay you. Better start packing your things for tomorrow. Here's some money for the bus fare, which you can pay back once you start working."

"But what will I eat, Father?"

"Don't worry, the mine company will feed you."

He put the money on the table and left.

There is an exhilirating experience, unparalleled by any other, in descending into the bowels of the earth. Perhaps death is as exciting but I still have to experience it. Climbing into the wire-mesh cage suspended from overhead cables was my first physical step towards mining. I boarded with nervous anxiety. Experienced workers smoked their pipes while others leaned against the seemingly fragile structure with looks of boredom on their dusty faces. I felt a sweat breaking out on my body. Perhaps it showed on my face, for suddenly I saw the others grinning at me. The operator released the handbrake and, with a woosh of air, we descended. The walls of the mine shaft seemed to rush in to us and the air became increasingly warm.

The cage stopped at various tunnel entrances. People came on, got off. Some had heavy, important-looking equipment all covered in dust. A few times, young white men in neat white dust coats came on board holding clipboards and pencils like badges of office. They rarely spoke to anyone or each other. When we finally stopped at our tunnel entrance, I was surprised to see the cage going down even farther. The deafening roar of jackhammers came from the well-lit tunnel. Even though it was unbearably hot, I broke into a cold sweat.

The work was back-breaking. However, I felt a new strength developing within myself. Swinging the pick or pushing the jackhammer, I worked with the frenzy of a man possessed. Afterward, showering in the cement cubicles, I would feel a quiet sense of fulfillment enveloping me. At first I was anxious to display my knowledge of the world and the people and things in it. Later it became a burden which I soon learned to abandon lest people avoid me because they thought I was trying to be different from them. Sometimes older men would ask me to read or write a letter for them. Otherwise my education was like a beautiful teapot which gathers dust on the shelf and is only taken down for the benefit of visitors. Slowly and imperceptibly the stories of Napoleon, Waterloo, spyrogyra and the annual rainfall of the Amazon basin receded from my memory. I no longer even thought of Sister Eileen and her English countryside. Only sometimes did the memory of my mother appear. One day I was startled by the thought I could no longer remember what she looked like. I simply couldn't remember her face. Sometimes, before I fell asleep, I would see her face vaguely but, try as I did, I could not bring her features into sharp focus. On other occasions, there would be the outline of her dress hem and her gnarled, swollen feet in fashionable shoes. But like an aging conjurer, I could not bring her full picture into view.

And then, two years later, the shift boss told me I would be laid off at the end of the month.

I pleaded with him to let me stay. I told him there was no work at the mission station; I had no relatives living. All to no avail. My passbook was stamped to say I was no longer employed in the area and had to leave within twenty-four hours. Thrown out of the company hostel, I had nowhere to sleep.

There was no one living at the mission station. The principal's house was empty. The classrooms that once were alive with children reciting math tables were now as quiet as death. Desks upended, papers and books strewn on the floor and a dried puddle of blood in a corner—these were the only signs of a hasty, violent escape.

Later the soldiers came. They frisked, arrested and interrogated me. The two hundred Rands I had saved was taken. After six months of beatings and imprisonment, I was released. What else could I do but come back here?

David Haidimbi has asked me to join the guerrillas but I cannot go into another unknown. Their slogans of freedom, equality and justice are strange words in my ears. This is where I make my last stand. From this place I will not leave; somebody will have to kill me first.

There is an order to my life now. While all is still dark outside, I get up from my sleeping place behind the altar and await the arrival of the soldiers. I pick up every shred of paper and stuff it into the neck of my shirt. My trouser pockets are too full now. One day, when I have time, I will read all these pieces of newspaper, hymn books, letters and bills brought here by the wind. Perhaps they will give an answer to my life and the meaning for my continued existence.

FOR MY DIARY

THERE WERE FRESH REPORTS OF RENEWED VIOLENCE IN THE townships this morning. The radio announcer also said that from somewhere beyond South Africa's borders, a certain banned organization, until recently unknown, had claimed responsibility for the bomb that killed an old and crippled white woman in the supermarket last week.

I write all these things down in my diary. One day I want to write a book about these events. It will be a very readable book. Not a thriller or a collection of statistics but a personal account of events as they unfolded and what I was thinking at the time. I even include other people's thoughts and the clothes they wore on a particular day so as to put things into proper perspective. For my information I do not depend on the newspaper. Instead I listen very closely to the news on the radio. Although the state controls the radio entirely, it is far easier for me to dismiss the half-truths and half-lies that assault my eardrums. I have become such a good listener that I can sense a lie coming just by the tone of the announcer's voice. With the written word it is far more difficult to separate fact from fiction. The lies are embroidered in such fanciful headlines as to mislead the most serious, honest reader. It is immaterial whether the paper supports the government or the opposition. Both parties have their reasons for distorting the truth. I have this distinct notion that both employ massive computers to churn out their ideologies in various formats to suit the different papers. You could say that my diary is closer to me than my husband is. Perhaps Paul doesn't understand the reason for my daily entries now, but he will when I come out with a book after all these troubles are over.

I was quite surprised at work this morning. On my way to the managing director's office to get some contracts signed, I saw this tall, blond white man talking to the receptionist in the foyer. I was almost past them when he called out loudly, "Hi, Alice! Do you ever look smashing!" Thinking it was some company sales rep getting fresh, I ignored him and kept going. For an instant the voice had sounded familiar but the man seemed a total stranger.

"Don't you remember me?" he called again. "I'm Dave. Dave Witzenberg." I stopped and turned. "We met at a student conference in Stutterheim in '68, remember?" The man was almost pleading for recognition now. He made a few steps toward me and then I realized who he was.

I stretched out my hand in a formal greeting and he gave me a clammy handshake. "Are you the same Dave who sang and played the guitar that time?" I asked.

"Yes." He beamed. "You told me then that you were from Paarl but I never thought I'd run into you here. What a surprise!" He was going to hug me but I dropped his hand and stepped back deftly.

The beard was all gone now. Only a well-trimmed moustache covered his upper lip. The jeans, sandals and shoulder-length hair were replaced by a pinstriped, three-piece business suit and handstitched, black moccasins. An expensive cologne wafted across to me. I noticed in his eyes that I had also made it. His gaze took in my stockinged legs, drifted upward to the tweed skirt and rested on the chiffon blouse. I crossed my arms and held the sheaf of documents in front of me.

He said he'd worked two years at Marks and Spencer in the U.K. after graduation. "Did you also get to go overseas?" he wanted to know.

"No," I said. "I just came back home and started working at this place."

He looked pointedly at my left hand. "So you're married now? Any children?

"Only two," I replied, hastily adding, "boy and a girl. Four and two years old." On an impulse I felt like riling his complacent, well-fed look. "Why are we discussing all these petty bourgeois issues? Have we changed so totally that questions of national liberation, the emancipation of all people and," on stepping closer to him, I whispered, "the overthrow of the racist regime have become totally irrelevant?"

His knuckles grew white on the handle of his briefcase. "I thought you were serious about leaving the country for guerrilla training," he said.

"Of course I was serious," I countered, "but new priorities have come up and surely life must go on. Even revolutionaries have to earn a living. "Trying to keep control of the conversation, I said, "You seem to have done well for yourself, Dave." Perhaps I should have cut the conversation short with a quick, "See you around then," but I was hoping he might say something profound for my diary.

"So what are you doing here, Alice?" he wanted to know.

"I've been chief assistant buyer for the company for the past six years," I answered.

He affected a British expression: "Well, jolly good show," and suddenly we were lost for words. I had wanted to ask him what position he now held with his father's company but felt it was a waste of time. Who was he to talk about guerrilla training?

During that conference in Stutterheim he'd never shown any of the radical commitment most had displayed. Once he'd supported a motion to have white universities opened to all races. Another time he had even seconded my motion for universal adult franchise for all South Africans. However, when it came to congratulating the Cuban government on the successes of their latest five-year plan or endorsing the struggles for freedom in Moçambique, Angola and Guinea-Bissau, he neither participated in the discussions nor voted on the issues. He either remained silent or abstained from voting. While my parents had scrounged and saved to put me through the University of the Western Cape, his father had been grooming him for a position with the family's department store chain.

I wondered whether I should ask him about some of the student leaders at that conference like Karl Tip, Helena Bezuidenhoudt or Auret Pretorius. Living in this country town has completely cut me off from mainstream politics. Sometimes I see their names in the English medium press. This one banned for five years. That one awaiting trial on terrorism charges. Did he know that Jeanette Curtis had been killed by a parcel bomb in Angola last month? One of the most brilliant, incisive minds I ever came across. And yet with all that intellectual power she was always painfully honest in her deliberations. Unlike me, she'd had the courage to leave this country and take up the struggle from outside.

I noticed the white receptionist staring pointedly at me as if she didn't like seeing me talking to a white man. "You have a message or something for me, Miss Emily?" I asked this over Dave's shoulder in Afrikaans.

She blushed. "No, nothing really." She busied herself with the switchboard.

Dave looked at me quizzically.

I fumbled for words to part graciously and half-turned to leave. "Sorry, but I have to go now."

But he wasn't ready to let me go. "What time do you have lunch?" he asked, unnecessarily loud.

I turned back and answered, "From one till two."

"Could we have lunch together this afternoon, at Le Parisien?" He looked at me appealingly. The man was a fast mover. Hardly in town, and he already knew which white places had been opened for blacks. But what right did he have to invite me? We hadn't had a strong relationship of any kind, neither as youthful radicals nor as lovers. Instead of making some flimsy excuse, I nodded a mute yes. "At one o'clock then?"

I muttered agreement and rushed away from him with my heels tapping too loudly on the parquet flooring. Why was I feeling so strange about this lunch meeting? White men had never held any special attraction for me. Although quite a few company reps made passes at me, I knew how to put them in their places. Even when Dave was strumming his guitar at parties, his appeal had been entirely artistic — I had concluded in hindsight. A few times he did hold my hand, but that was only when we sang that we shall overcome and for God to bless Africa.

Back at my office, I sensed word had reached the manager about my meeting in the lobby. I saw him fumbling with a file behind my desk. "Just checking on the General Electric contract," he explained. "It's due to expire soon," he added while paging aimlessly.

"Not for another six months, sir," I said. I had caught him lying and his wrinkled jowls took on a reddish color. I wondered whether to tell him about my lunchtime appointment. Not so much for his permission but to set the record straight in case some people misunderstood the whole thing. But surely it amounted to the same thing as asking for permission? I decided to play it all by ear. His next statement came as no surprise.

"You seem to have some pretty powerful friends, hey Alice?" He grinned. "Boyfriend or something?"

I tried to sound nonchalant. "Just somebody I know from my student days, Mr. van Rensburg."

"You two studied at the same university? Must've been a fair bit of hanky-panky going on there." He leered at me. How could the man be so stupid? Of course I had had to go to a black university.

"No, sir," I said. "We were just members of the same student movement." Did I use the wrong word? "Movement" sounded so political. "Organization" seemed more tepid. "At one time," I added. I motioned that I wanted to get back to my desk.

He continued paging through the file. "Must've been a bunch of radicals, you fellows, trying to change the world in one day. Overthrowing the government and having a Communist revolution." I sensed another of his sermons about having been raised the hard way through correspondence schools and working himself up by his own boot strings.

"Sorry, Mr. van Rensburg," I said, "but I have to make a call about some rewound motors. The engineering department has been screaming for them all morning." I made a grab at the telephone and started dialing.

Halfway to the door he turned and shouted, "Next time leave your chit-chat for after company hours! I'm the one who gets shit for your goings on!"

I got an engaged signal and redialed the number. To hell with the so-called name of this company. I was not going to ask anybody's permission to have lunch with a white man.

What were Dave's real intentions with this invitation? Was it an on-the-spur-of-the-moment goodwill gesture, or was he trying to make up for ten years before, when he was too occupied with his own perspective of student politics to have much time for sex, or was he simply being nice? Perhaps it made good business sense to take a client company's employees out for dinner these days. But then apartheid is still firmly the law of the land — not counting the cosmetic changes — and at this company everybody toed the line. I thought of mentioning the lunch appointment to van Rensburg after all, but since he knew I had been talking to a white man, surely Emily at the switchboard would've told him too about this date.

In the bathroom mirror I brushed the kinks out of my hair until it shone with its own dark brown sheen. It's been weeks since I've been to the hairdresser and the straightener is beginning to wear out. To hell with it, I decided after a few minutes. It wasn't as if I were preparing myself to meet God or King George. Rabia's entrance startled me. I'd completely forgotten about her. She was a bright little typist.

"You going out for lunch?" she wanted to know. "Sorry but it's the first day of Puasa, fasting time, right now. Otherwise I would've gone . . . "

"No, don't worry," I cut her short. "I understand. See you later, hey!" And I left her behind in the washroom. She obviously knew nothing about my lunchtime appointment. I decided to tell her the whole story later. As an unwritten rule we always went out together for take-out lunches. Now her month of fasting made it easier for me.

I felt a little apprehensive when we pulled up outside the restaurant. For one, I'd never dined in the company of whites and secondly I felt I was compromising my political beliefs in black consciousness by being there. The doorman gave Dave a beaming nod but simply stared through me. Noticing this, Dave took my elbow and steered me into the foyer. After a few moments the maitre d' led us to a corner table. By the looks from the other tables I could see I had made Dave very proud. A few white men, in the company of their wives, were even staring openly. Dave pulled out my chair and seated me with a flourish the other men obviously envied. Between the foyer and the table I had been reduced to just so much breast, hip and thigh. In my moments of self-awareness in public, my first thought is always how men — any man — might possibly view me. Have the values of this society become so corrupted that even I value myself first and foremost in terms of my ability to provide pleasure?

Somebody at one of the other tables noticed I was married. An old Boer woman in a flowery print dress, with diamonds on her fingers, whispered loudly in Afrikaans to a beanstalk of a man in a safari suit. "Surely she can't be his wife! The law doesn't allow it. Maybe she's just wearing the ring to cover up, I tell you!"

From another table came a fresh attack in the same language. This time from a woman with a round, well-fed face. "I know these Coloured whores! No respect for themselves or anybody else at all! Now they're even plying their trade right amongst us!" From the corner of my eye, I noticed the maitre d' rushing fleetfootedly in the direction of these tables with a terribly worried look on his face. I felt I should just get up and leave but I didn't want to give these racists the idea they could chase me out of there. Dave seemed totally oblivious to what was being said around us. But then, I suddenly remembered, Afrikaans was not his first language. Mistaking my depression for anxiety, he tried to set me at ease with an earlier question:

"So what have you been doing since you've left university?"

Before I could reply, the headwaiter appeared with two menus and asked if we would like something from the bar. Dave mutely deflected the question to me and I, my knowledge of wines and liqueurs evaporating under stress, named a popular beer currently advertised by black wrestlers.

"You're sure?" he asked while the waiter grinned.

"Yes," I replied. I folded and refolded the large, white, damask napkin in my lap.

The waiter brought the beer and again deferred to Dave. In a further attempt at gallantry, he motioned the man to serve me first.

"So, you're still not married," I ventured. I sipped at my beer.

He spoke about live-in situations and affairs in such a detached way it sounded as if the women had been cars he had leased. Finally, having exhausted his little repertoire, he lifted his beer glass in a mock gesture of celebration. "To our meeting again after so many years."

I added conspiratorially in hushed tones, "Hasten! The revolution!" He blinked as if wondering whether I were a member of some ultra-leftist revolutionary group. "It was one of our drinking salutes in '68, remember?" We chinked glasses.

He fell silent again. Success in business had obviously not changed the inner man. He was still reticent.

"A penny for your thoughts," I prodded.

He looked up, surprised, and took a quick gulp from his beer before speaking. "I saw in this morning's paper that there was a flare up on the Cape Flats again. Things still quiet in your neighbourhood?"

I hesitated before replying. Did this man think I was living in the ghetto? After musing for a minute, I decided he was no different from the two white women with their openly racist remarks. How could he possibly group me and my neighbourhood with the bunch of ragtag stone throwers he had seen in the paper? I considered giving him a lecture on manipulation of the capitalist media. Instead I replied noncommittally, "Oh, it's still very quiet, but people in my area are not really given to stone throwing, you know."

Our food arrived. Dave got his Greek salad and I was served chicken cordon bleu.

"Remember Algeria?" he suddenly said. "Soon we won't be able to do this." He waved to include the entire restaurant. "These sorts of public places were the prime targets of the FLN. Throwing bombs and grenades at a frightened civilian population."

I couldn't let him get away with this oversimplification of the state of affairs of our country. I set my knife and fork on the side of my plate and finished chewing behind my hand. He stopped eating politely. "There are similarities between the Algerian revolution and current South Africa," I said. "But surely the struggle here is not to drive an occupying colonial force out of the country?" I let the question hang in mid-air.

"And they didn't burn their own people alive with petrol-soaked tires either," he countered. He signalled the waiter to bring another two beers.

Did I have to explain the ramifications of these gruesome deaths to a fellow countryman? Did he want me to concede that the struggle for freedom was now out of the hands of an organized liberation movement given only to the blowing up of bridges and power stations? That the township thugs had seemingly taken over? I wanted to tell him the necklacings were as remote from my life as from that of somebody living in Switzerland. However, the fear that I might be seen as betraying even the victims of these gruesome deaths left me mute.

He looked up from his plate and emitted a hasty, "I'm sorry."

Damn all this skirting around issues, I decided. I was not going to let him get away with this. That beer had made me reckless. I aimed my voice over his head at the Boer women.

"For apartheid to work," I said while getting up from my chair, "the whole state machinery depends on the black township police, community councillors and networks of informers to kill and harass opponents of the system." I knew I was on dangerous ground for insulting these Boers, but I had never had the chance to tell whites what I thought of them and their system. In a louder voice I continued. "Besides, you are the people who keep me oppressed! You keep apartheid alive with your racist remarks! You're to be blamed that people get burned inside motorcar tires! But your turn will come! I swear to God!"

A Boer woman restrained her husband at a table close by. It was time they realized they were living a lie. It was enough I had to live by the restrictive codes of conduct to earn my daily bread. There I took my stand.

Dave looked at me with a mixture of anguish and surprise. "Maybe we should continue this conversation somewhere else," he whispered. He motioned for the bill.

"I didn't start this!" I replied.

The maitre d' suddenly appeared at my elbow. "Sir," he ordered condescendingly, "I must ask you to leave!"

Outside, Dave looked as if I'd embarrassed him through some unmentionable act. "You want a drive back to the office?" he asked unnecessarily.

"No, I still have some shopping to do." I was not prepared to carry this charade any farther. "Never mind, Dave, I'll take a bus."

"Well, see you around then," he said. He got into his sports car.

There were still a few factory girls milling about the gates when I got off at the bus stop nearby. In the foyer, Miss Emily ignored me totally. There will be fresh scandalmongering about me, but at least they'll say the white man refused to drive me back because I wouldn't have sex with him. I can live with that.

THE LAND OF OTHERS

AGAINST THE STARLIT SKY MELVYN GROEPE SAW A LAZY WISP
of smoke spiralling from a chimney a few hundred feet away. In the
past he would have walked over for a chat and a smoke to that
house. Not now. Everything had changed.

Instead of the Willemses for neighbours, he now had squatters
living on the next farm. Overnight they had appeared. Without
furniture, trucks or anything. He never saw any of them arriving.
He woke in the morning and found them there. Nothing to mark the
usual signs of human habitation, like washing on the line, a cock
crowing or the laughter of children playing; only the parents (or
what looked like adults) silhouetted in the unframed, smashed-in
windows. Like guilty ghosts the figures retreated into the dark
interiors. The five farms between his place and the
Cathcart-Seymour Road were now filled with squatters. It didn't
take him too long to find out. A simple drive in the early evening
had shown the telltale spirals of blue-grey smoke. Otherwise, there
was no sign of life during daytime. Pretty stupid, he'd thought, to
give themselves away like this. But then, he brooded, since they
were people (even of the lowest class) then they surely needed the
heat at night like everybody else.

He wished his former neighbours hadn't been so spineless as to
move out at the first hint of trouble. Overnight they had
disappeared. One day he talked to a man; the next day he was gone.
Once or twice Melvyn had stumbled across somebody who was
getting ready to leave but they had given him no explanation and he
hadn't asked any. It was enough he'd seen them all packed and
ready to leave. Now this. He should have spoken about the
squatters at tonight's meeting. It would have been easier for him to
talk about their taking over land they had no rights to. Instead he
had gone to the meeting with ideas of fighting the government.

Melvyn ignored the sounds around him as he fished for his cigarettes in his breastpocket. He struck a match and cupped his calloused hands around the flame through force of habit. Exhaling the first breath of languid smoke, he stretched his legs and adjusted his bony frame on the wooden bench. Three rows away he saw Valerie and William Englebrecht sitting huddled together. She dwarfed her husband. They were the parents of that boy who had made Josephine pregnant. After a few moments of intense staring, Melvyn got William to look his way. Following immediate recognition and a brief nod, the man dropped his eyes. They were supposed to have come over and talk about the children tonight. With this meeting they obviously couldn't. Well, Melvyn decided, these people obviously carry the shame for their son's randiness. And rightly so. After a minute he pushed them from his mind. He was getting frustrated with the way the meeting was going, but he stopped himself from adding his voice to the angry chorus. Crossing one creased pant leg over the other, he took the situation in again. With so much tobacco smoke in the dimly-lit school hall, he could hardly make out the people in the front benches. Only the tall speaker was clearly outlined, under a solitary bare electric bulb.

This was not the way Melvyn had thought the meeting would go. The few times he had attended meetings of some sort, they had been orderly affairs. At such times the chairman would say a few words and be followed by various people offering their opinions. Depending, of course, on how much the speakers knew about the subject under discussion. This, this was pure madness.

His own plan had been to speak as soon as Hendrik Hendricks finished reading the government proclamation. Melvyn had no fancy words with which to attack the official document and its flowery language. He was simply going to ask why Hendricks had allowed himself to become a spokesman for the government. Couldn't it send its own people to tell the community to leave because Coloureds could no longer live here? The idea struck him that Hendricks was betraying them all by doing this dirty work. Then Melvyn dismissed the notion. Perhaps Hendricks felt it was his duty to bring the message, however bad, to the people. Perhaps, instead of asking a question, he could simply say it was not a good thing for Oom Hendrik to bring the message. He should return the document to the government officer and say nobody here wanted to lose their land. This way, Melvyn thought, he could get the support of the community without seemingly going to war with Hendricks over his position as leader. He could see in his mind's eye how the people of the valley would rally around Hendricks to defy the government order.

Melvyn looked about the dense mass of people huddled in their thick winter coats. Was there nobody else here with a similar idea? He wondered what the aged Oom Gysman, sitting close to the front, thought about the meeting. Melvyn had never had much dealings with the man and couldn't say he knew him that well. Unlike Oom Gysman, Melvyn had never had a voice for meetings and speeches as such, but he had hoped, perhaps prayed more than hoped, that he could summon the courage to speak a few words. He felt his sense of orderliness slipping away in the cacaphony of voices. He couldn't even think straight it seemed. The women's shouts of dismay cut like rusty knives through the gutteral protests of the men. He felt himself getting very hot and coughed a few times before taking another puff.

He had spoken to Linda but she didn't have too much to say except, "So now you're trying to attack Oom Hendrik. It's not enough that the Boers are driving us out of this place. Now you have to go and fight over who should be speaking for the government. Lord help me, I'll never understand your reasoning!" That was two weeks ago. She had misunderstood, but he hadn't bothered to explain himself. The urge to speak now filled his insides so much, he thought he might burst. He took a last puff and stomped out the butt on the cold cement floor. Now it seemed too late to say anything.

The lamentations of the obese Valerie Engelbrecht broke through his pondering. "Oh Lord," she cried, "what's going to happen to us?" She raised her right hand for permission to speak. With a shudder she lifted her bulk and continued in a quivering voice. "Oom Hendrik . . . Oom Hendrik . . . I . . . I do not have many words . . . " Her voice threatened to break and, with a shaky hand, she pulled a laced handkerchief from her handbag. After a few sniffles and dabbing of her eyes, she continued in a stronger tone. She eyed upturned faces squarely.

"What I want to say is this, Oom Hendrik. For all these years we, our parents and their parents before them . . . we have been the most law-abiding community. We worked for our daily bread and we paid our taxes. And for what! For what have we lived such model lives that the government has to come and uproot us now? Look at this meeting. There is not half the three hundred familes who are supposed to be here. Where have they gone? And I want to ask you something else. Did we come here to be told what the government's plans are or what? I for myself came to this meeting tonight so that we can look at something with which to fight this expulsion order and not to be lectured to. My schooldays are long gone, Oom Hendrik. You can teach my children, but my days for schooling are long past." As an afterthought she clenched the handkerchief and pointed her finger at the chairman.

She sat down with such vehemence that the bench emitted a loud creak. There were immediate guffaws, which were drowned by thunderous clapping. An uneasy silence followed this outpouring of support. A grudging respect took hold of Melvyn's insides. Valerie had not only voiced his opinion but she had probably spoken for the whole meeting.

So now he had squatters on his hands.

He had made no attempt at even acknowledging their presence. From their side, there was only an elusiveness. From their looks he could see they knew very well they had no right to be here. Their children were, of course, the most noticeable. During the first day of moving in, settling down or call it what you will, the parents would manage to keep the children indoors. It was a different matter after that. In torn rags, the urchins would peer around the corners of the houses. They would be intent on making some sign of friendship to the children in the area. His own children quickly got wind of where he stood with squatters and viewed these half-cringing, half-brave attempts of communication with disdain.

He was having some problems with Lizzie, though. At nine years old she was growing precociously into her teens. Always had been a serious-minded child. Always wanted to look neat and composed and never allowed herself the shrill laughter and silliness of others her own age. Once he'd caught her swearing softly while the squatters' children made faces at her from the other side of the fence. She was on the verge of throwing a rock at them when he'd stopped her. There was really no point in getting into a fracas.

But how did these people live, he asked himself. It remained a mystery where they'd come from and how they had existed. There never was any of the industry that marked human habitation, like a woman doing the wash or a man going to work. A few times he'd seen the children buying half a loaf of bread at the village grocery store. That seemed the extent of their subsistence.

He veered toward the chicken coop and the hens clucked in alarm. At the back he found a wide, gaping hole. Stretching the mesh wire, he hooked it onto the protruding nails. Linda had mentioned she was missing a few hens but there was nothing he could do about it. First he had toyed with the idea of hiring one or two of the squatters (this way, at least, he would have earned a sense of loyalty from them and they would not have become chicken thieves), but he knew the community would have his blood for such an act. It would have legitimized the squatters' presence.

Melvyn was on the point of speaking when Hendricks cleared his throat. Barely a few feet separated the thickset old man from the sea of humanity. He had to hand it to Oom Hendrik. The man certainly had the guts to face this concerted anger without a sign of weakness. Except for occasionally wiping his bald pate with a starched white handkerchief, the man showed no outward emotions. After Valeries's outburst and during the applause he had turned his gaze to the nearest window to stare at the inky darkness outside. He seemed to be treating them like a bunch of rebellious school children. The silence, which had become unbearable for just about everybody, seemed to be the signal for Oom Hendrik to take the initiative.

Like a spring released from tension, he jumped from his chair. He threw the documents on the table with a flourish and stepped in front of it. Some of those in the first rows shrank visibly from this direct affront and cowered among themselves.

In a sudden surge of ill will, Melvyn wondered how much the old man was getting paid for putting up this performance. He reminded himself he was not intent on crucifying the messenger, but why was it this self-imposed leader had shown no sympathy with them? He was a Coloured person like everybody else here but he was not merely content with bringing the message; he was trying to whip the people into shape to accept it. Hendricks's incisive voice cut through Melvyn's thoughts:

"According to the government proclamation, this land of the Kat River Valley did once belong to the Xhosa people. To quote from the document again . . . " He leaned back, took the sheaf of papers, shook it and, squinting through his bifocals, started reading. " 'It was only through the benevolence of the late Queen Victoria's government that this area of the Kat River Valley was given to the Hottentot captains who had defended the Eastern Cape frontier during the early nineteenth century after taking it from the Xhosas.' So, there you have it, people. The government is basing its expropriation on the ancestral rights of the Xhosas and the repulsion of treaties that were made, according to them, with a foreign government. Which today has no say in the internal affairs of this country, South Africa." With another flourish he pocketed his bifocals and set the papers neatly on the table behind him. Now he leaned against the table and invited people to put their questions to him.

Melvyn had made up his mind. This man, this retired school-teacher who had always lorded himself above everybody else, had never had a stake in this valley. For as long as Melvyn could remember, the man had always prided himself on his origins in Cape Town. As a teacher he had simply lived off the fruits of the villagers' toil. It had meant nothing to him whether he had been a teacher here or somewhere else. Why was it that this man, who had always reckoned himself to be the most educated in the valley, had not thought of some plan to counter the government action? He simply gave them an interpretation to official decisions made thousands of miles from the Kat River Valley. As a community they had had no say in those decisions. Melvyn's mind raced again as he sought for suitably eloquent phrases with which to express his frustration.

For almost fifty years Hendricks had been teaching the children of this rural community. Like Melvyn himself, most of the parents here had been educated by the seventy-five-year-old. Most of them, if not all, had gotten a thrashing from him at one time or another. Melvyn got more whippings than he could recall. Of course Hendricks hadn't always been an old man; still, the very notion that he had taught and thrashed them seemed enough to instill confidence in him. Through the smoky haze, he was attacking somebody in the front row:

"I'm telling you that this order comes from the central

government in Pretoria! Do you want me to read it to you again?" Hendricks reached behind him, set his glasses on his nose and, after a moment of searching, found the relevant passage. "Can I have some silence here!" he thundered. "I called for this meeting and while I'm in charge, you will listen to me!"

An uneasy quiet again crept through the hall. A few women in tightly bound headscarves stifled their whisperings, while here and there a pipe smoker waited poised for the next verbal barrage.

"Okay," he continued, "the proclamation states that this area of the Kat River Valley is to be ceded to the Ciskei Government of Chief Lennox Sebe on 1 May 1987 AD. All Coloured inhabitants of this valley will be compensated by the central government for their properties here. Do you understand that?" Receiving no reply, he shifted his attention to Oom Gysman. "Yes?" Hendricks took his chair again. Melvyn knew that, in any other society, Oom Gysman would have been revered for his age and his link with the past. Only among Coloureds was his presence a reminder of a past they would much rather forget about. More than that, he was a living reminder to them of their aboriginal origins. Aided by two buxom granddaughters, Oom Gysman rose to speak.

Melvyn turned from the chicken coop toward the cattle *kraal*. He was walking so far now that, on looking back, not even the light in the kitchen window was visible. The homestead was just a blurred outline against the starlit sky. A cow nosed up to him and nuzzled his hands for salt. After he sold all his cattle, he would have enough to build himself a decent house somewhere in Cape Town, East London or Port Elizabeth. There wasn't really a market for all his farm machinery, because the only way he could get rid of the old was to buy new stuff. This had been the tradition ever since he remembered his father farming.

He knew each of his animals by sight. With an effort he brushed the regret from his mind. All those twenty young heifers he had planned to breed with Gert Jacob's new bull. Well, life was life. Now he had an eighteen-year-old who was bred by some reluctant stud. Melvyn had had the strange, perhaps crazy urge, to ask Josephine how it had happened. He knew he would never get the full story as to how she had become a woman. Perhaps an odd word here and there from Linda, but the full story would forever remain a mystery.

Of course, he'd never spoken to Valerie and William about the affair himself. Most of what he knew came from Linda's mouth. For himself, if he'd had his way, he wouldn't have cared one shit about the whole thing. If he'd had his way, he would have put the child up for adoption and sent Josephine back to school. But women always seemed to have the final say in these things.

Women's business. That's what it was. He could only imagine what had happened and how. Somewhere, in a secluded spot Josephine, the one who was going to be the first teacher in the family, had removed her panties and allowed a good-for-nothing to ravish her. To mount her like a bull and penetrate her. Repeatedly. How many times did they have sex before she became pregnant? The question stopped his train of thoughts. He smashed his fist in the palm of his hand. This was no way for a man to think. A man who called himself a man didn't dwell on such things. This is craziness he reminded himself. It was like fornicating with his daughter in his own mind. He swore softly and remembered the beating he had given Josephine. But he had done his *vaderlike plig*, fatherly duty, and he had done it in Linda's presence. He had given Josephine such a beating as she had never had in her whole life. What more could he do to punish her?

"Meester Hendricks," Oom Gysman stormed, "what I want to ask is this. Is there nothing that we can do to stop this, this handing over of our land to the Xhosas? I speak now of Toeka's days," and he paused for a minute, "but my grandfather and other leaders in the Rebellion of 1854 showed the government that they wouldn't take things lying down."

Melvyn sat up straight to listen. This old man with his heavy, plodding Afrikaans, rich with the accent of the old Khoikhoi language he could still speak, was referring to a past which was despised by nearly all present. However heroic it might have been. In their clamour to be accepted in the white man's world, they were willing to trample and destroy everything that reminded them of that past. Melvyn caught Hendricks knitting his eyebrows in sudden anger. He was about to say something, but the Oom Gysman continued in his halting, rasping voice:

"Teacher Hendricks . . . and . . . you my people—" He flung

both arms wide to include the entire gathering. "I am talking now of things that you do not know and things which you, *almisque*, do not even care for. I tell you that people died in that Rebellion of 1854. But even though . . . even though they died, the land remained in our hands to this day. And now you simply want to run away. I tell you . . . I tell you that nothing comes to you without a struggle."

Respect for Oom Gysman had stopped Hendricks from interrupting him earlier, but he was now going too far. "That's enough, Oom Gysman," Hendricks said. "Thank you very much. Is there anybody else who wants to speak?"

"But I haven't finished . . . " the old man croaked again.

Hendricks's voice had grown hard. "You can sit down now. We have to give everybody a chance to speak, Oom Gysman."

Assisted by his granddaughters, who were embarrassed by their grandfather's outburst, the old man took his seat with reluctance.

Melvyn knew that what Oom Gysman had said was probably true, but one needed a stronger person for such talk. To most people, what the old man had said was entirely inconsequential. However, Hendricks clearly saw him as a threat. Hendricks spoke again:

"No, Oom Gysman. There is nothing that we can do to stop this government order. This is a step by a government that is far removed from us. If there are any amongst you who are even thinking of drawing up petitions and such things," and he paused to take in the whole hall for added emphasis, "then I will tell you that I will have no hand in such things whatsoever. These things, as you well know, always bring out the worst part of the government. Do you want to see us here invaded by soldiers and police, shooting and killing us? We're not a bunch of riffraff or skollies. We are law-abiding citizens. When I came here to this valley in 1935, there was nothing here." He paused for a minute and kicked back his chair. From his new position he now continued in a far more authoritative voice.

"This community was busy dying. Just about everybody was suffering and seeking escape by running away to Cape Town, East London, or Port Elizabeth. There a far worse fate awaited them, living cheek to jowl with criminal elements. But after that, after my arrival, in a Christian spirit of law-abiding citizens we built this community together. No, Oom Gysman, at my age and your age we do not want to see the fruits of our work destroyed by a stupid act of revolt. Your grandfather may have revolted in 1854, but what did it bring him? What did it bring him but the death sentence!"

Oom Gysman stared at Hendricks throughout all this tirade. Melvyn felt sorry for him now. The glowering looks from the other benches were telling Oom Gysman he was to blame for this outburst by Hendricks. A hush had fallen over the meeting.

Melvyn decided he had had enough. The bravest thing he could possibly do now was to walk out.

Even as he got up, nearby whispering voices fell silent in anticipation that he, one of the leading farmers in the area, was finally going to speak. People shifted in their seats while he purposefully strode toward the front of the hall. Some wondered what was happening when he avoided the chairman's table and made for the door. Hendricks shouted before he could leave:

"But the meeting isn't over yet, Melvyn Groepe! We've still got a lot to say! Like how we're going to sell the farming equipment and livestock! We want to leave here like champions! Not like running dogs!" He was pleading for respectability in the face of tragedy.

For the barest moment, Melvyn felt indecisive. Did this man now expect him, who stood to lose the most, to sit quietly and discuss his own downfall? Was the man so concerned with orderliness that he did not realize how much pain it caused to lose one's land even if you got paid for it? This was more than a question of land and money. It was a whole way of life that was being destroyed. Finally he summoned his courage. "Oom Hendrik!" he shouted, pointing his finger at him. "I've said nothing tonight at this meeting but what I want to say is this! After so many years among us, you have always prided yourself on not being from here but from elsewhere." He paused to regain his composure. "After so many years, you are selling all our faith and trust in you down the shit pot." Melvyn slammed the door behind him on the muted cacaphony rising inside.

In the gloom of the paraffin lamp, Linda sat at the kitchen table darning a sock. Through a flurry of curtains, Melvyn saw Josephine, heavily pregnant, disappearing into her bedroom.

"But you're back early," Linda said without lifting her head. "How did the meeting go?"

He heard the smaller children snoring in one bedroom. In silence he poured himself a mug of coffee and drew a fresh cigarette from the cigarette holder. He took a seat opposite Linda and sloshed half the coffee into a saucer. After slurping from the saucer and drawing on the cigarette, he spoke in a flat voice. "Oom Hendrik is selling us down the drain." He said it quietly and waited for her response.

"What are you saying there?" She looked up from her needlework.

"You've heard me right," he said. He gulped another mouthful of coffee.

"But how can you say such a thing?" Sudden alarm raised her voice a pitch. "Surely you're not serious, my husband!"

"*So waar die Here*! As true as God," he thundered. A little coffee spilt onto the table. "What do you think when the man says that we have to start arranging how we're going to sell our livestock? Lord God Almighty! Gentle Jesus!"

She winced at the double profanity and got up to grab a rag from the sink. With a quick, deft motion she wiped the table clean and stood waiting for him to speak.

He continued in a quiet voice. "I think the best that we can do is to pack up and leave."

She turned to face him squarely. "But after all these years of working and toiling here?" She let it hang in mid-air.

"No, I tell you Linda I'm just gatvol of that bloody Hendricks and his tricks. Through all these years, he never allowed anybody to do anything without his say-so. What happened when we wanted to start a co-operative here?"

She dropped her eyes to the floor.

"What happened when we wanted to start a political party here? No, he would say, we don't need these things. We have always lived in peace. Political parties and co-operatives are for those who want to fight the government."

"But why are you bringing up all this?"

"You'd better understand me clearly, woman. Because what I'm going to say now, I will not say again!" He held out his mug and she poured him a fresh cup. "You know why that bloody Hendrik Hendricks didn't want all these things here? Because he wanted to be the only one in control. And look now! Just look now! We need a strong leadership to hold the people together, and there is *bleddy* well nothing! Fuck-all I tell you. Only this fucking Hendricks to bring the government's message to a bunch of sheep."

"But isn't there anybody else among the men who can see your point? It's late to start those parties and things now, but isn't there anybody else among the men?"

"In that whole entire meeting, there were only two people who spoke up. And do you know who they were?"

"No, my husband," she said. She settled her slim figure in the chair opposite him again.

"Well, I'll tell you. The one was Valerie Engelbrecht and the other was the aged Oom Gysman." After a minute he continued. "No, my wife. There are too few people to counter this influence of Hendricks. As for us, the best thing is to pack up, sell our stock and leave. I know that there are some who will try to bribe the new Xhosa rulers in trying to let them stay on. But what happened to them who tried to stay on in the Transkei? They gave gifts of cattle to the new rulers but finally they had to leave with only the shirts on their backs. By order of Pretoria. I am not planning to leave here *kaal gat*, bare assed. I've had enough of all this and tomorrow I'm driving over to see a few white farmers in Fort Beaufort." The cigarette died with a hiss in the coffee mug.

"But we were all born here, my husband. Both us and our children and even our parents and their grandparents knew no other home." She remained quiet for a minute and then continued as an afterthought. "And there's still the question of Josephine. We're getting ready and Valerie and William were going to come and talk tonight if it weren't for that meeting!"

He thundered across the table into the darkened bedrooms, "Josephine!"

A meek, sleepy answer of "Pa?" came back to him.

"No! No!" Linda protested vehemently. "Don't upset the child now. You know she's already in her seventh month and she's carrying very badly."

"Well, who told her to go and get —"

Linda cut him short. "Don't you come with the self-same story now, Melvyn!" Her earlier docility was suddenly replaced by a fierce protectiveness. "What has happened, has happened." Measuring each word carefully, she continued in a precise and even tone. "We. You and I. We will do our best to save the situation. No matter what happens or what anyone says. This is our problem and we'll do the best we can." She picked up the mug and rinsed it furiously under the tap. After a minute she continued in a quieter tone. "And don't forget yourself eighteen years ago, Melvyn Groepe. My parents also had great plans for me."

He avoided her stare and stepped wordlessly out of the kitchen. In the cool evening air he heard the village clock strike twelve times while he walked toward the barns.

With this government eviction order on his mind, he hadn't had a chance to give Josephine's pregnancy too much thought. As a matter of fact, he hadn't thought about it at all. Well, at eighteen she was old enough to get married and set up a house of her own. Only this boy of the Engelbrechts (Melvyn had never had much time for these people) was now saying he wanted to qualify for something first before getting married. Some excuse about wanting to give Josephine and the baby a better life once he had a trade. "It didn't take any qualifications to get his pecker up," is what Linda had said. Well, Josephine had certainly disappointed him. As the daughter of one of the well-to-do farmers in the area, and with the good looks she'd inherited from her mother, Josephine could have had a far better choice than these good-for-nothings.

Melvyn started walking slowly back in the direction of his house. In the kitchen there was still some warmth from the wood stove. The coffee pot was empty and cleaned for the next morning. There was still some hot water in the kettle. A sudden thought made him reach for the bottom drawer of the kitchen dresser. From a crumpled brown paper bag came the smell of *boegoe*. He was not really feeling sick. Tonight he simply felt tired to his bones. He stuck a piece of firewood among the glowing embers and drew the kettle closer to the heat. He'd always associated the smell of the boegoe herb with sickness and poverty. Normally it was only the very poor people, who couldn't afford to see a doctor, who used the traditional herbs. But Linda, with her old-fashioned ways, wouldn't let go of folk remedies. She would even gather up the dust from the doorstep and smear it under an infant's nose (she called it giving the child the smell of the house). He had always had enough money to see the best doctors, but he let her have her way. Well, he decided, as he put a handful of the brittle green leaves into the coffee pot, he could think himself traditional too. He added some boiling water to the *boegoe*. After all, he'd always spilt a little liquor for "the old people" before his first drink. The bitter, mustiness of the herb enveloped his senses as he took the first scalding sip. A sense of well-being flooded his body.

AN ELECTION

AS USUAL, HER VOICE CARRIED THROUGH THE CLOSED SCREEN door while she was busy in the kitchen. It was the hot summer of 1984 and he had been canvassing this poll for the past two months. He always lingered by the backdoor of this house to talk with the woman. He never went inside. She never came outside either.

"But do you really think our notion of long-term aid is all that effective?" she asked. "I mean, here we export all this industry and technology to the developing world. Do they really need it?" She ran the tap briefly while she waited for his reply.

He countered gently. "From what I've heard, most of the developing agencies like CUSO or the USC simply respond to what the people in Africa and elsewhere want for themselves." Through the screen door he could see her peeling potatoes. Her movements were swift and economical. She rinsed, squared, and again rinsed the four pieces while reaching for a fresh potato with the other hand. Brushing a stray blonde hair from her forehead, she continued in her slow, measured tone: "I know that. But the final decisions are still made in Canada's boardrooms. Did you see the story on "The Journal" about that bakery in Tanzania? We built the bakery but now the bread's too expensive for the poor people. Only the rich Tanzanians can afford it."

He didn't really feel like arguing with her. There were still too many Canadian issues he felt uncomfortable with. Besides, he'd grown so fond of her that he didn't want to see her angry. That was why he responded lamely with, "No, I do feel that the decisions are made on humanitarian grounds and obviously people will make mistakes. The best intentions always carry a margin of self-interest and error."

"Perhaps you're right," she said. "You're not just saying this to make a white Canadian feel good, eh?"

"No, ma'am. I do believe that Canadians, on the whole, have a concern about justice and equality in the Third World and ARTHUR is no exception."

There was a plonking sound when she emptied the bowl of potatoes into a saucepan. "As our federal representative he's quite good," she said. "He speaks very well on social issues, especially uranium mining and nuclear proliferation. On the Third World, he definitely lacks depth."

He couldn't remember how this conversational relationship had developed. They'd said so much every week that if anybody had asked him now what was spoken during the first conversation, he would not have been able to remember. Yet, despite the heat, she never offered him a refreshment. Perhaps she didn't want to create the wrong impression. There were the neighbours, after all. Nobody else on Matthew Street offered him anything either. Still, he'd expected her to be more progressive than the other people in the neighbourhood.

He rested his eyes on her bare, painted toenails briefly before meeting her inquiring gaze. In her mid-thirties, she still retained some of her youthful good looks. There was a fullness to her lips, heightened by slightly protruding upper teeth, which gave her whole appearance a look of innocence. In the cool semi-gloom of drawn blinds, her deep-set green eyes conveyed the image of one at peace with herself. He wondered how she got the tan when she always seemed so busy indoors.

Two months before at the citizenship ceremony, the charge by the presiding judge had been that he, among several new Canadians, should become involved in the political process. Now, after five years in the country, he felt comfortable enough with the political milieu to canvass in this poll. Most of the houses had neat, well-kept lawns, with vegetable patches in the backyards. His impulses to stereotype the homeowners, however, immediately disappeared when the front door was opened. In dress and appearance, some women resembled characters in the soap operas. A few times there were tiny, shrivelled old ladies shrieking above the noise of hysterical poodles that they were no longer interested in politics. Or, prodded on by a toothless old Baba, families with strong Eastern European looks and musical names would declare their devotion to the party. Then there were the young mothers, trying to cope with two or three toddlers as well as a new pregnancy. Morning, afternoon and evening, there was always a woman to answer the door. The men were busy — at work, reading the paper, cutting grass or just getting drunk in front of the television.

In the old country of South Africa, he had never been allowed to vote in parliamentary elections let alone work actively for a political candidate. Now in his early thirties he was doing exactly what he had long wanted to do. Walk from door to door and tell people about the cause he believed in without fear of arrest or police harassment. Of course, having been founded only a year ago, the party was small. Still, like the party, he felt himself growing politically each new day. Who could say? Perhaps one day he might even stand as a candidate himself. Some people said he already sounded like a politician. And yet this new society had given him the beginnings of a paunch. In five years he'd never had to haul water, gather firewood or walk six miles to town. He'd never seen any overcrowded classrooms or heard of somebody dying because there was no money for the doctor. All these and more were taken for granted. He missed the mountains of his hometown, though. He wished he had told her about the valley, the changing seasons. Now there was no time for any such talk. Tomorrow was election day and all this common interest in a national event would come to an end.

Drying her hands on a towel, she leaned with her hip against the door frame. "How strong are we in this poll, do you think?"

He opened his file and showed her that of 223 eligible voters, 183 were party supporters of various degree.

"That's pretty good," she said. "What about the rest?"

"Well, about seventy per cent are opposition. The rest are undecided or have some beef about all politicians being corrupt." Suddenly there was nothing more to say. They both knew it. "I'd better be off," he said. "There's still so much to do with people needing rides tomorrow and so on." Grasping the poll sheets in his left hand, he made as if to leave.

"Well, goodbye and good luck," she said. "It's a pity you didn't get a chance to meet my husband. I told him so much about you." There was a finality to her words he couldn't miss.

He walked down the steps and wordlessly waved goodbye.

Five o'clock on the afternoon of election day, he was catching a break between driving people to the polls. Checking the voters' lists at the poll office, he saw she had already voted so there was no reason for him to go to her place. Maybe he could find an excuse. He could just tell her he'd noticed she hadn't voted yet. If she said she had, then he could ask her to come to the victory celebrations. Simple as that.

He drove over to her place. There was nobody in, not even the docile husband she had described so vividly. A man devoid of his own political views. Hard-working and a good provider to judge by the degree of comfort.

He scowled at the screen door. Was it part of his desperate desire to be accepted in this society that he had to chat up married women? He couldn't remember when he had last laughed at himself. In the country of his youth, he'd had many friends. There, friends were people to whom your poverty or wealth didn't matter. There you were simply liked or disliked because of your character. Here he only had acquaintances, people with whom he shared interests. He returned to the car, switched on the ignition and reminded himself to be stong. This new country had brought new possibilities, some of which he'd never dreamt of. But then these brought their attendant responsibilities. He would have to pray to be strong. Forget about this married woman and the meaningful conversations he'd had with her. Better not go to her house again, ever. She wasn't the only person with whom he discussed politics. There were many others in the past and there would be even more in the future.

He brought the car to a slow stop at the poll office. Getting out, he suddenly realized there were only thirty minutes left before the polls closed. He checked his poll sheets. There were eleven recalcitrant voters left. Not really party faithful, but still people who had indicated a willingness to vote for ARTHUR. Inside he found two women hard at work at a kitchen table. Poll sheets, party signs and papers were strewn over the floor. He addressed himself to the closest woman: "Cheryl, I've still got eleven voters outstanding. Can you check and see if any of them have voted yet?"

"Sure thing. Give me the poll number and read out the names."

He was left with seven names of people who had to be taken to the poll. An idea struck him when a young man came into the office. "Hi, Paul! Good thing you're back. I've still got a few outstanding voters."

"So what do you want me to do?" Paul sounded exasperated.

"Let's go together in my car. Drop me off at the first house. If the person needs a ride, you take them to the polling station while I walk to the next house. Got the picture?"

"Sure thing. Let's go."

In the car he copied down the seven addresses. He felt good about what he was doing now. It kept his mind occupied.

The first house presented no problem. The couple had been working all day and their car was in the garage for repairs. He immediately showed them there was a car waiting outside to drive them to the poll. At the second home he told the old gentleman to watch out for a green Volvo station wagon which would return from the poll shortly to pick him up. There was a problem at the third house, though.

The single mother had three children. "No," she said. "I'm not going to let you baby-sit for me."

"Well, can't you take them to the poll with you?"

"No, I can't."

"Just hang on right there, ma'm," he said, running out the front door. Back he ran to the first house. Thank goodness: the first couple had already returned from voting. "Mrs. Brandon," he gasped, "I need your help very badly."

"Yes, what is it?" she said.

"We've got a lady five doors down," he stammered breathlessly. "She needs a baby-sitter so she can get to vote."

"Well, if you reckon we're gonna win by one more vote, I'll sure do it."

While he ran ahead of her, he saw his car approaching. The old man from the second house was returning from the polls. He got out of the car gingerly and started walking back to his house. "Thankyou, Mr. Jewel!" he shouted after him. The old man merely nodded in response and shuffled along.

Mrs. Brandon had hardly got into the car when he slammed the back door shut. He took a seat in front and directed Paul to the next assignment.

In a short while they arrived at the house where the woman needed a baby-sitter.

"Here, ma'am," he said. "I've got a baby-sitter for you."

Embarrassed, she handed her baby to Mrs. Brandon and got into the car.

When he checked his watch he saw there were five minutes left before the polls closed. No point really in pursuing the other voters. He started walking back to the poll office.

A girl he'd seen before was busy sweeping the office floor. "Where has everybody gone?" he asked her.

"To the victory celebration I guess," she answered. She resumed her sweeping. She didn't seem talkative so he lit a cigarette and made himself comfortable behind an empty desk.

Soon his car arrived. He asked Paul if he wanted a ride to the celebrations.

"No thanks. I'd rather go home. I'm too tired after this long day and I'd rather catch it on TV."

"Well, okay then. And thanks for the help."

"You're welcome. See you around, eh!"

"Sure thing."

Starting the car, he was of two minds. He didn't really feel like going home now; on the other hand, he just couldn't stand the idle chatter of parties. He thought of his shabby, two-room apartment and the long night ahead. He'd probably get homesick again and toss around in his bed all night. No, the presence of any human company would be better than that apartment. He finally decided to go. Perhaps he would run into somebody familiar at the celebration.

The hall was crowded with people, smoking and drinking. Every wall was covered in charts displaying polls in the constituency. On a newly erected stage, the candidate and his family were being interviewed by CBC. ARTHUR's teenaged children seemed very ill at ease in this sudden glare of limelight. Only his wife was excited about all the attention from the TV cameras.

A pretty, dark-haired woman in peasant sandals and headscarf sidled up to him. "Who do you think is going to win?" she asked in a throaty French accent. She added as an afterthought, "Are you a member of the party or just a supporter?"

"Oh, I do my little bit," he said. "Besides, I like the idea of a fair distribution of the country's wealth. Of course, I hope to see something similar in my own country one day."

"Oh yeah?"

"Sure."

His eyes darted around the room as he tried to find the woman from Matthew Street. After a while, he decided there was no way he was going to find her in this crowd. He tried to make himself comfortable with this woman's company. She seemed a little bored so he offered her a refreshment.

"Would you like a drink?"

She brightened. "A gin and tonic, please."

After he returned with the drinks, he made another attempt at conversation. "Well, what brings you to this part of the world? You are from Quebec aren't you?"

"Yes. I'm just here for summer vacation."

Should he talk about the PQ or the FLQ? Maybe it was passé to talk about the FLQ. Almost twenty years had passed since the Emergency. Then, perhaps the PQ was no longer relevant. He didn't want to start something he couldn't finish or say the wrong thing and embarrass himself by it.

Sensing his indecision and discomfort, she excused herself, mumbling something about "washroom."

He stood about staring aimlessly for a minute. The charts on the wall got his attention again. Of the 223 eligible voters in his zone, he saw that 152 had already been counted for his candidate. Surely there must be somebody in this hall with whom he could share the good news. Looking around, he saw the French-speaking girl in conversation with a young blond man dressed in a black sweatshirt. Their heads were close together and, as he watched, the young man hugged the girl.

He left the crowd of enthusiastic revellers behind and stepped into the chill night air. Overhead, a few strands of clouds drifted to the west. Tonight he didn't feel like locating the Big Dipper even though it always reminded him of the Southern Cross. He didn't even want to get drunk to hide his loneliness. Tonight he simply felt like dying. With a loud curse he tried to shake himself free of the despair. He could see her sitting in front of a small black and white screen mumbling agreeably while her husband commented on the outcome of the polls.

ARCHIE CRAIL

Crail is the author of numerous plays for theatre and radio. *Exile* (Blizzard 1990) was produced by Twenty-Fifth Street Theatre of Saskatoon and is currently being adapted by the author into a feature-length film script. Crail is writing another play for Twenty-Fifth Street Theatre entitled "Beyond the Kat River." The National Film Board of Canada has commissioned him to write a feature-length film entitled "Birdsong" and CBC's "Ambience" has commissioned a radio drama, "For Better, not for Worse." Earlier plays include "Nistitum: The Gift" (1989), commissioned and produced by the Wolseley Historical Society; "Celebration" (1988), commissioned and workshopped by Wheatland Theatre; and "The Awakening" (1986), commissioned and produced by the Southern African Solidarity Committee.

Archie Crail was born in Paarl, South Africa, and educated through the University of South Africa. He also spent two years at a theological college in Alice, Cape Province, where Bishop Desmond Tutu was his lecturer in Doctrine. Crail's political involvement during the seventies in South Africa with both labour struggles and the South West African People's Organization (SWAPO) forced his move to Namibia (formerly South West Africa) and his flight to Botswana. He came to Canada with his wife and four children in 1980. It was in Regina, Saskatchewan that he began writing seriously.

EMILE WILTON

Wilton was born in the "Mother City," Cape Town, South Africa in 1971. He was educated in Cape Town and Paarl and is currently studying graphic design.

Of his work Wilton says, "Cape Town and Paarl gave me a unique experience of two worlds. Art, for me, became a challenge to be met with intense emotion and concentration, not just being realistic in my work, but to improve oneself and with the task at hand."

COTEAU BOOKS

Coteau Books distinguishes itself among Canadian-owned literary publishers as the press that introduces prairie writers, especially Saskatchewan writers, to the English-language reading public. To obtain a complete catalogue of our titles please write to Coteau Books at 401 - 2206 Dewdney Avenue, Regina SK, Canada S4R 1H3.

Coteau Books has published a number of titles which reflect North America's cultural and ethnic diversity. These titles may be ordered from your local bookstore or directly from Coteau Books.

Batoche
by Kim Morrissey

Set during the North West Rebellion of 1885, *Batoche* goes beyond the bare historical facts. Morrissey has reconstructed history with the hopes and dreams of a people and the rumours and prejudices of an era. Batoche won a CBC Literary Award and was short-listed for The Lampert Memorial Award. Now in its third printing.

Poetry
ISBN 0-919926-91-6
$8.95 paper

Foreigners
by Barbara Sapergia

Foreigners is a novel about the struggle of one family to find its way in a new land. From Stevan Dominescu, the immigrant alienated from God and the Old Country, and his traditional wife, to Luba and Margaret, two strong young women of the new land—*Foreigners* is filled with lively and passionate characters. Sapergia draws on history and the memory of her own Romanian ancestors. Now in its second printing.

Fiction
ISBN 0-919926-35-5
$6.95 paper

Maria Breaks Her Silence
by Nancy Mattson

Maria Breaks Her Silence is a poetic biography of a woman from Kauhava, Finland, who immigrated to the New World in the 1880s. The poems explore her experiences as a woman through three marriages, the rituals of day-to-day life and raising two children, and as an immigrant in a new country. "Maria" is based on a real historical figure whom the author discovered while researching Finnish-Canadian history.

Poetry
ISBN 0-919926-93-2
$8.95 paper
ISBN 0-919926-92-4
$21.95 cloth

Out of Place
edited by Ven Begamudré and Judith Krause;
introduction by Alberto Manguel

Out of Place is an anthology of prose and poetry linked by the common theme of cultural displacement. The works of the thirty-seven contributors from across Canada develop different facets of this general theme; contributors range from the well-known such as Myrna Kostash and Kristjana Gunnars to new voices like those of Alice Lee, Michelene Adams and Doug Nepinak.

Fiction and Poetry
ISBN 0-55050-019-8
$14.95 paper

Pies
by Wilma Riley; illustrations by Sheldon Cohen

Pies is a humorous, full-colour picture book for children about neighbours from different "old countries" who argue about a cow. One plots revenge against the other by baking a "cow pie." After several funny incidents, everyone ends up friends and there is a subtle lesson about forgiveness and getting along with others, despite differences in backgrounds or cultures.

Children's
ISBN 0-55050-021-X
$6.95 paper